ROBBIE FORESTER

AND THE

OUTLAWS OF SHERWOOD ST.

PETER ABRAHAMS

ROBBIE FORESTER

AND THE
OUTLAWS OF SHERWOOD ST.

WITHDRAWN

PHILOMEL BOOKS
An Imprint of Penguin Group (USA) Inc.

PHILOMEL BOOKS
A division of Penguin Young Readers Group.
Published by The Penguin Group.
Penguin Group (USA) Inc., 375 Hudson Street, New York, NY 10014, U.S.A.
Penguin Group (Canada), 90 Eglinton Avenue East, Suite 700, Toronto,
Ontario M4P 2Y3, Canada (a division of Pearson Penguin Canada Inc.).
Penguin Books Ltd, 80 Strand, London WC2R 0RL, England.
Penguin Ireland, 25 St. Stephen's Green, Dublin 2, Ireland
(a division of Penguin Books Ltd).
Penguin Group (Australia), 250 Camberwell Road, Camberwell, Victoria 3124,
Australia (a division of Pearson Australia Group Pty Ltd).
Penguin Books India Pvt Ltd, 11 Community Centre, Panchsheel Park,
New Delhi - 110 017, India.
Penguin Group (NZ), 67 Apollo Drive, Rosedale, Auckland 0632, New Zealand
(a division of Pearson New Zealand Ltd).
Penguin Books (South Africa) (Pty) Ltd, 24 Sturdee Avenue, Rosebank,
Johannesburg 2196, South Africa.
Penguin Books Ltd, Registered Offices: 80 Strand, London WC2R 0RL, England.

Edited by Jill Santopolo. Design by Semadar Megged.
Text set in 12.5-point Bembo.

Library of Congress Cataloging-in-Publication Data
Abrahams, Peter, 1947–
Robbie Forester and the outlaws of Sherwood St. / Peter Abrahams.   p.   cm.
Summary: After getting a strange charm bracelet from a homeless woman, thirteen-
year-old Robyn Forester and new friends join together to fight injustice in their
Brooklyn, New York, neighborhood.
[1. Conduct of life—Fiction.   2. Justice—Fiction.   3. Magic—Fiction.
4. Neighborhood—Fiction.   5. Schools—Fiction.   6. Family life—New York
(State)—New York—Fiction.   7. Brooklyn (New York, N.Y.)—Fiction.]   I. Title.
PZ7.A1675Out 2012   [Fic]—dc22   2010042330

ISBN 978-0-399-25502-1
10 9 8 7 6 5 4 3 2 1

TO MY MAGICAL CHILDREN:
SETH, BEN, LILY, ROSIE

Many thanks to my wife, Diana, for the idea;
to my wonderful editor Jill Santopolo and my brilliant
agent Molly Friedrich; and to Josh and Maddie Cohen
for the generous gift of their time.

At first I thought it all began with a foul—if an elbow to the head's not a foul, then what is?—but I figured out, maybe not as soon as I should have, that the beginning had come a little earlier. Just five or six hours, in fact, with me on my way to school and no time to lose. The second the doors of the subway car slid open, I jumped out, hurried along the platform, and took the stairs to street level two at a time. At the top, I was turning left, all set to run the block and a half to school, when I noticed something not right in front of the newsstand by the subway entrance. A homeless woman who'd been sitting outside for the past few weeks—HOMELESS, PLEASE HELP read the writing on the coffee cup she always held—was out there again, only now she'd tipped over and lay on her side. It must have just happened, because none of the people around—and there were lots—had gone to her yet. So I did.

I leaned over her. The woman was old, with white hair and a lined face, but maybe because her eyes were closed, I suddenly had this vision of how she'd looked as a young girl. She'd been really pretty. Something about that took away the fear I'd normally have had at such a moment.

"Are you all right?" I said.

Her eyes opened—blue eyes, but so faded there was hardly any color at all, except for the whites, which were crisscrossed with red veins. "Do I look all right?" she said, her voice surprisingly strong and not at all friendly.

I didn't know what to say.

Her eyes narrowed. "I know you," she said. "You're the girlie who dropped eighty-five cents in the cup. And sixty another time."

My parents said not to give money to street people, that there were better ways of helping, which maybe made sense but didn't feel right. So all I thought at that moment was: eighty-five cents and sixty cents—not much.

"Sorry," I said, "but that was all I had on me and—"

Before I could finish, strong hands were pushing me to the side and voices were calling "Get back, out of the way." Two cops had arrived and were clearing space around the woman. I ended up behind some tall people. An ambulance came roaring up, siren blaring. I caught glimpses of EMTs hopping out, feeling her pulse, clamping an oxygen mask over her face, rolling her onto a stretcher, and hoisting her into the back of the ambulance. The crowd lost interest fast, everyone dispersing, giving me a clear view, and what I saw was the woman's arm dangling down from the stretcher and something slipping off her wrist and falling into the gutter. I went forward and picked it up. It was a braided leather bracelet, possibly a charm bracelet, although only a single charm hung from it—a tiny silver heart.

"You dropped this," I called, just as the ambulance doors were closing. No one inside noticed me, except for the woman. Her eyes were looking right into mine and seemed to be trying to send some message, but I didn't get whatever it was. The doors slammed shut, and the ambulance took off. I ran a step or two after it before giving up. Then I put the charm bracelet in my pocket and hurried to school.

The foul I mentioned before happened after school on the basketball court, and real fast. Real fast was how things always happened on the basketball court, the mental part, too. Final seconds ticking down, Welland 18, Thatcher (that was us) 16, a typical score in the Independent School League, Seventh and Eighth Grade Girls Division, "independent" being a nicer way of saying "private." The games went by in blurs, partly because of the speed and partly because Dr. Singh, my ophthalmologist, didn't believe in fitting kids for contact lenses before they turned thirteen and I wasn't about to wear my stupid glasses on the court, since that meant wearing those even more stupid safety goggles over them. Did that mean I'd rather let my team down than look like a bug? If so, I'd have to live with it.

Back to the foul. In this particular blur, a component blur within the blur of the whole game, Ashanti, our tallest and best player, had intercepted a pass and cut across the key, a step ahead of number ten for Welland, who was even taller. But as Ashanti rose for the shot, number ten leaped, too, twisting in the air, elbow up, and that elbow caught Ashanti smack on the forehead. And right in front of the ref, a chinless guy with sharp, darting eyes whom I'd seen around the neighborhood but couldn't place at that moment. Right in front of his sharp, darting eyes: impossible to miss, but no whistle, no call. What was up with that?

"Hey!" I yelled.

Oops. Yelling at the ref was a complete no-no, also a technical, and in all the years I'd been playing basketball, now almost three, I'd never heard a player do it. But it was so obvious! And wrong! The ref didn't seem to have heard my yell—he was missing everything, an equal-opportunity goof-up—and meanwhile things were happening, such as Ashanti starting to fall, the ball coming loose, and big number ten turning to chase after it. Somehow the ball came bouncing right into my hands, out in three-point land.

"Shoot, Robbie, shoot!" That was the coach, Ms. Kleinberg, shouting at me from the bench. She'd played for Dartmouth and even tried out for the Olympic team, getting cut in training camp. Ms. Kleinberg had a fantastic shot; I'd seen her hit forty-seven in a row from the free-throw line. But shooting wasn't my thing. Passing was my thing. I always looked to pass the moment I got the ball.

But no one was open, at least no one in my field of vision—not a very clear field, on account of my unaided eyesight, minus three in the right, minus two-point-five in the left.

"Shoot!"

I just stood there, felt a sweat smear on the ball, not mine, since I hadn't yet worked up a sweat. This was actually the first time I'd touched the ball in the second half. I was a seventh-grader and new to Thatcher and not a starter, and also didn't deserve to start—don't get me wrong about that. In the first half, I'd come in with about five minutes left, made two successful passes, and been called once for traveling, probably adding up to my best performance of the season, so far. For some reason, Ms. Kleinberg had decided to push her luck and send me back in at the end of the game, crunch time. Since then, I'd mostly been running up and down the floor, never too far from the ball but also never a factor. I was fine with that; I liked running.

Number ten closed in.

"Two seconds! Robbie! Shoot!"

Two seconds? Not a good moment for weird distractions to be happening, but a weird distraction was happening: suddenly my head hurt, my forehead, in the exact same spot where number ten had elbowed Ashanti. Was *pain* even the right word? This . . . *feeling,* maybe a better name, was like a tiny low-powered electric ball. It seemed to be pressing just behind my forehead, pressing, pressing, and then with no warning, two tiny electric currents seemed to emerge, one hooking up to each eye, and the pain, or feeling, vanished immediately. And all at once, my vision cleared, and I could see perfectly, more clearly than at any time in my life, every detail sharp and focused! And not only that—

Number ten was almost on me, her long arms up, hands high.

"Shoot!"

And not only that, but I saw—or thought I saw, since it was so impossible—the strangest thing: a narrow beam of light, reddish light, very faint, with golden highlights, that seemed to glow right out of my eyes. It shaped a long, rising arc, then sloped down into the basket, dead center. Somehow I knew it was no longer a matter of shooting the ball—normally so big and unmanageable— but simply lofting it up onto that red-gold glowing beam. So I did, just lofted the ball onto the beam. The beam vanished at once, and then there was only the ball, soaring over number ten's outstretched hands, curving through the air with lots of backspin, just like a shot launched by someone who knew what she was doing, and then—*swish*. Nothing but net, from three-point land.

Bbbbzzzz. The buzzer buzzed. Game over. Thatcher 19, Welland 18. A buzzer beater? I'd just won the game with a buzzer beater, like in the kind of daydream fantasy I didn't even have anymore, at least when it came to sports. The kids were around me now, pretty pumped, although not too pumped, which seemed to be the Thatcher way.

We went into the locker room. In my old school, PS 501, the Joe Louis School, there hadn't been a locker room—the kids made do with the bathroom near the gym—but the Thatcher girls' locker room was nice, with a steam bath, individual shower stalls, fluffy white towels.

Ms. Kleinberg patted me on the back. "Nice job," she said. "More, more, more."

"Um," I said, giving Ms. Kleinberg a careful look.

Now that the excitement, what there'd been of it, had died down, I had a chance to think, *Hello? That beam, red and gold? Anybody?* But nobody said a word about it. Meaning no one else saw it except me? Whoa.

"No foul?" said Ashanti, kicking off her shoes. "Is he blind or something?"

"That's life," said Ms. Kleinberg, handing her an ice pack. "Have a good weekend, everybody. Practice Monday." She went into her office.

Ashanti sat in front of her locker, dropped the ice pack on the floor, gave me what seemed like an angry look. "An elbow in the head is life?"

"Does it hurt?" I said.

"What do you think?" said Ashanti.

Ashanti was intimidating, but a question I thought was important had occurred to me, so I pressed on. "Does it feel kind of like a tiny electric ball?"

Ashanti squinted at me in a scary way. "Huh? Is that supposed to be funny?"

"No," I said. "No, no." I moved to my own locker, which looked out of focus, meaning my vision was back to normal. I took out my glasses and put them on. Very cool glasses from the Smith Street Eyeware Boutique, one of the coolest opticians in Brooklyn, which probably meant in the whole world, but I hated them. Other ophthalmologists handed out contacts left and right. How come I got stuck with Dr. Singh? And as for the red-gold beam, either some new eye screwup was in the mix, or I'd imagined it. What other explanation was there? No one had seen it: therefore, not real. The imagination played tricks on you. That was one of my dad's big beliefs. He was writing a novella about it, or possibly a memoir.

I closed my locker, glimpsing my face in the mirror that hung on the inside of the door. Nonna—the name for Grandma that my grandmother on my mother's side had finally chosen for herself, after tryouts for Mummymum, Nana, and Gretchen (her given name)—had gazed at me on her last visit (she lived in Arizona and didn't visit often) and said, "She'll be a beautiful woman, one day." Kind of a mystery who Nonna had been addressing, since there'd been just the two us in the room, but that wasn't the point. The point: was this supposed day coming anytime soon, the day of my beauty revealed for all to see? No sign of it yet. I clicked the combination into the locked position and was turning to leave when I felt a strange warmth in my pocket. I reached in and took out the braided bracelet. The tiny silver heart was more than warm—in fact, almost too hot to touch. My locker was near the heating vent: maybe that was the explanation. But that silver heart was kind of pretty. I slipped the bracelet on my wrist.

• • •

Home was two subway stops away, but it was a nice day—nice for winter, meaning sunny, not too cold, and none of that wind funneling through the gaps between buildings and down the streets, like icy invisible streams— so I started walking. Twenty-two blocks—twenty-five if I took a detour past Joe Louis—from the edge of one cool neighborhood, where the adults looked a lot like my parents, through the main portion of the walk where they did not, and finally to the edge of another cool neighborhood, mine, where they did again. The difference wasn't skin color—Ashanti, for example, lived practically across the street from me—or the manner of dress, although that was part of it; it was more something else, some attitude thing, much harder to define.

I passed some nice brownstones, the fixed-up kind with freshly painted trim, nothing crumbling, plants in the windows. Two nannies stood in front of one of them, each push-pulling on a stroller, back and forth, back and forth, in a machinelike way. The babies slept, one drooling, one not. Then came a grocery store with brightly colored fruit in the window, all arranged in neat rows. I crossed the street to the first block where walking at night wasn't a good idea, passing a boarded-up building, a warehouse, an old greasy sofa in the gutter. A veiled woman with just a little slit to see through went past, her dark eyes lighting on me for a moment. Rowdy boys on bikes blew by, fluttering the veiled woman's robe. My backpack got heavier—there was homework at Thatcher, lots—but I turned left at the next corner and took the detour anyway. Not that I liked going by Joe Louis, exactly; it was more a matter of just being drawn to it.

It was past dismissal by the time I reached my old school, a brick and glass building of no distinction, very different from Thatcher, which was a grand nineteenth-century affair on the outside, bright and modern on the inside, thanks to the work of a famous architect who was also an alum; there were lots of famous alums from Thatcher.

Some of the kids from my neighborhood got sent to private school right from kindergarten; others made the switch later—third grade, maybe, or fifth. But the plan had always been for me to be a public school kid from start to finish; my parents believed in public schools. "Just wait," some of their friends had said. I'd heard that plenty of times. My parents had waited and waited and then been in the very last group to cave. Nothing I said or did had budged them, and I'd thrown everything I'd had at them, emptied out the cupboard of bad behavior. "Your friends from Joe Louis will still be your friends," they'd told me. Which had already turned out to be false. And "Don't worry—you'll make new friends at Thatcher." Which hadn't happened yet, most of the Thatcher kids having been there together for years. Didn't mean it wouldn't happen, I told myself, stopping by the chain-link fence and gazing through at the small, paved school yard with its single backboard, no net on the basket, windblown trash and broken glass heaped in the corners.

No one was shooting hoops. There was only one person around, a kid I'd seen in the halls. What did they call him? Tut-Tut? Yes, that was it, on account of his stutter. He'd arrived from—Where was it? Haiti?—two or three years before, a scrawny kid with modified dreads and a sweet face. Right now he was squatting down on the pavement just a few feet from the fence, drawing with chalk. Tut-Tut didn't seem to notice me at all; I could feel his concentration. He shifted around a little, and I saw what he was drawing.

Hey! It was beautiful: a red bird, maybe a parrot, with a green head and yellow eyes, so lifelike that it looked as though it could actually fly off the pavement at any moment.

"It's great," I said.

Tut-Tut glanced up, startled. He almost tipped over backward.

"Is it based on a real bird?" I said.

Tut-Tut's mouth opened, and his lips moved a bit, like he was forming a word, but no sound came out.

"Or did you just make it up?" I said.

"N-n-n-n-," said Tut-Tut. "T-t-t-th-th-th-th . . ." He went silent.

"It's real?" I said.

"T-t-t-t-th-th-th-th-the b-b-b-bb-bb-bbb-bbbb-bbbbb-bbbbbb . . ." He went silent again, took a deep breath, and nodded yes.

A real parrot, meaning it had a name, maybe a parrot he'd seen in Haiti, or even kept in a cage. I had lots of follow-up questions, but I didn't have the heart to watch Tut-Tut trying to answer them. Plus, that strange pressure ball thing in my head was back, not electrical and powerful like on the basketball court, more just letting me know it was there.

Tut-Tut licked his lips. "W-," he began. "W-w-w-w-w-w-w-wh-wh-wh—"

The pressure thing grew. And the more Tut-Tut tried to say whatever it was he wanted to say, the stronger it got. "W-wh-wh-wha-wha-wha-wha-wha—" Now I felt the electrical component, and my vision started going funny. My imagination playing tricks? I took off my glasses, watched the world grow clearer.

"Wh-wha-wha-wh-wh-wh-w-w-w-w . . ." Tut-Tut gave up.

And the moment he gave up, my vision began deteriorating back to normal. The pressure in my head vanished. I put on my glasses. If this was my imagination, it was suddenly getting good at tricks. The streetlights went on.

"I better get going," I said.

Was I coming down with something? I took off my glove and touched my forehead; it felt cool. And in fact I felt fine all over, head to toe, the way you do after running around for a while. There were also growing pains to factor in: lots of possible explanations for something that would probably never happen again. "Anyway, cool bird," I said.

Tut-Tut grunted.

I walked off. A block away, waiting for the light to change, I felt the silver heart. It had heated up again, but now cooled quickly under my touch. The light changed. I glanced back. The school yard was empty.

I t was almost fully dark when I turned onto my street, climbed for a couple of blocks, and reached the top of the slope. The western view opened up: the river, which still somehow had a glow to it, like it was clinging to daytime; the Brooklyn Bridge, looking like it was built of lights alone; Manhattan. A million-dollar view, which was probably an underestimate. People said a million dollars weren't what they used to be; maybe it would be better to go back to when they were. But that was off topic, the kind of mind wandering that kept me from being a straight-A student, according to my first-term report card, or getting any A's at all, the grading at Thatcher turning out to be much stricter than at Joe Louis.

The best part of the view, in my opinion and maybe mine alone, was how it disappeared behind the nearby buildings slice by slice and piece by piece on the way down the other side. Hard to explain why, and also off topic. I headed down the street, passing Local, the new cool neighborhood bar, and Zimmy's, the used-to-be-cool neighborhood bar, then Au Boulot, the bistro that had been cheap until it got a great review, I couldn't remember where, and Monsieur Señor's, the coffee place where my dad sometimes worked when he got sick of being alone at home. And there he was at one of the window tables, espresso cup in front of him and laptop open—although he didn't seem to be working, instead was talking to a guy at the next table, also with espresso and laptop. He saw me, smiled, and waved me inside. I went in—the air always so different from ordinary air, like landing on planet Coffee—and walked over to Dad's table.

"Hey, there," he said. "How was your day?"

"Good."

"Shep," he said, turning to the other guy, "this is my daughter, Robyn. Robyn, meet Shep van Slyke."

I shook hands with Shep van Slyke, remembering too late that maybe you were supposed to take off your glove first.

"Shep wrote that book you loved so much when you were little," Dad said.

"*One Snake, Two Snakes*?" I asked. An important book for me: it had taught me how to count, for one thing, and not to fear snakes, for another.

"No, no, no," Dad said. "The one where everybody's a baker."

"*Too Many Pies*?" I said.

"Yeah."

I turned to Shep van Slyke. He was watching me kind of intently, like . . . like, was he waiting for me to say something about *Too Many Pies,* some kind of compliment?

"Um," I said, no compliments coming in time.

Shep van Slyke blinked. "I'm a fan of *One Snake, Two Snakes,* too, Robyn," he said. "And—"

"Robbie."

"I'd be interested in what you liked most about it."

"The pictures, I guess," I said. "I really liked your pictures, too," I added, which was true, although for some reason the story in *Too Many Pies* hadn't grabbed me. Not even the story, so much, but the . . . what was the word? Started with *C.* I couldn't come up with it.

"My pictures?" said Shep van Slyke.

"In *Too Many Pies.*"

"I didn't do the pictures."

"Oh."

"Just the text," he said. "And the concept, too, of course."

Concept: that was the *C* word I'd been searching for.

Shep van Slyke glanced at clock on the wall. "Look at the time." He folded his laptop and rose. "Keep in touch, Chas," he said, and to me, "Nice meeting you."

"Bye," I said. Shep van Slyke wrapped his scarf around his neck and left. I sat down next to my dad.

Hugh, the barista who was in the middle of having all those tattoos removed, called over, "Hi, Robbie. Hot chocolate?"

I glanced over at my dad; he nodded.

"Yeah, thanks," I said.

"And an espresso for me," Dad said.

Hugh brought over the espresso and a mug of hot chocolate, much darker than the hot chocolate you usually see and without the whipped cream swirl on top; whipped cream swirls weren't the style at Monsieur Señor's. I took a sip—steaming, not too sweet, delicious. I didn't have a sweet tooth, took after my mom that way. Over the rim of my mug I watched Dad stirring sugar into his cup. I had a very young-looking dad; his face pretty much unlined, his hair without a touch of gray, always sort of scruffy, like a college kid who'd just gotten out of bed. He was turning forty next fall.

"He's not such a bad guy," Dad said.

"Who?"

"Van Slyke. Disney's looking to turn one of his books into a movie."

"*Too Many Pies*?" I couldn't see how you'd make a movie out of that.

Dad shook his head. "A new one—it's not out yet." He sipped his espresso. "His agent's one of the best."

"Oh," I said. My dad was between agents right now, exactly how and why not too clear in my head. But I knew agents were important from conversations I'd overheard my dad having with other writers. They talked about agents a lot, way more than the stories they were dreaming up. "How's the novella going?" I said.

"It's actually more of a memoir, but with a fictional interface, clearly distinguishable, of course."

I failed, one hundred percent, to understand. My dad was a brilliant writer, had already published two books. The first one, *All But the Shouting,* had come out the year I was in kindergarten, and . . . what was the expression? Made a splash? So books that failed made no splash, just sank to the bottom? And books that succeeded made a splash and then sank to the bottom? My dad's second book, published last year, was *On/Off,* a huge novel, over a thousand pages, that I'd heard him calling "kind of an experiment, in retrospect" on the phone not too long ago.

Memoir was about memories, right? "Memories of what, Dad?" I said.

He smiled. My dad had a very nice smile, except lately there'd been some question about tooth grinding in his sleep, and now he needed some implants. And wasn't he supposed to go easy on those late-afternoon espressos?

"That's what I'm working on now," he said.

I was confused. "You're working on the plot, Dad?"

"*Plot*," said Dad, making air quotes around the word, "is problematic. I'm talking about what and who the memories will be attached to. In other words, I'm starting with pure memory and working back."

I had trouble following that, but at the same time, it reminded me of scenes in *Alice in Wonderland* and *Through the Looking-Glass,* so it couldn't be all bad: those books had sold in the billions! At that moment, Dad's eyes shifted, a look I was long familiar with; it meant he was getting an idea. He turned to the laptop.

"Finished your hot chocolate?" he said, fingers gliding toward the keyboard.

"Just about. I saw this homeless woman lying on the sidewalk today."

"Oh?"

"They took her away in an ambulance."

"Probably just dehydration," Dad said, his fingers now on the keys. "Pendleton could use a walk."

I drank up, rose. "Are you coming?"

"After I make a note or two."

I knew that those notes, even one or two, could take time. "See you."

Dad nodded.

I walked home. Home was only a block and a half farther down the hill, an apartment that took up the top two floors of an old brownstone. There were two heavy wooden doors at ground level. The one on the left led to Mitch's apartment; he was the landlord, worked on Wall Street. The door on the right was ours. I unlocked it, climbed the steep staircase to the inner door, unlocked that, too. I could hear Pendleton whining—or possibly crying, the family not being in agreement on what to call that sound—somewhere inside.

I closed the door, double locked it, shrugged off my backpack, which hit the floor with a dishearteningly heavy thump. "Pendleton?" I called. "Where are you?"

The whining or crying stopped.

"Pendleton?"

No response.

"You've done something bad, haven't you, Pendleton?"

Nada.

"And now you're feeling guilty."

I heard him on the stairs to the top floor, meaning he'd been in one of the two bedrooms—mine or my parents'—or possibly the tiny bathroom up there.

He came around the corner, into the living room where I could see him. Yes, bad and feeling guilty. The thing with Pendleton was that doing bad and feeling guilty about it often happened at the same time for him—more than once, just watching him, I was pretty sure he sometimes actually felt guilty first. Another thing about Pendleton was how often he was the first to provide the evidence of his misdoings, sort of cop and perp in one body; one huge body in his case. Right now, for example, he was dragging along my dad's favorite bathrobe, soft white terrycloth with the words *Hotel Amanjena, Marrakech,* stitched over the chest pocket, a pocket no longer quite attached.

"Pendleton!"

He turned away, but didn't go anywhere. His head swiveled back to give me a sheepish look. Maybe not the right word, *sheepish,* since sheep were probably fiercer than Pendleton. But never having been close up to a sheep, I couldn't be sure.

"Drop it."

Pendleton sank down to the floor, rolled onto his side.

"For God's sake." The fabric had gotten hung up on one of Pendleton's teeth, not a first and no surprise at all, on account of how enormous his teeth were. I knelt down and got everything untangled, then held up what was left of the robe. "Realize the kind of trouble you're in? Look what you've done."

Pendleton showed no interest in doing that. Instead he stuck out his pink tongue and gave me a lick.

"That won't work with Dad," I told him. I rose. "Time for your walk."

This city was full of dogs cooped up all day who couldn't wait to get outside. Pendleton wasn't like that. He preferred the indoors, only wanting to go out when he was desperate, and he was capable of holding on for amazing amounts of time. I took the leash off the door, hooked it to his collar.

"Up."

Pendleton didn't move, just lay there on his side, tongue hanging out a bit, eyes vacant. I tugged on the leash, couldn't budge him. "All right, all right—you can have a treat."

He bounced up—maybe not bounced, but he did rise of his own accord—and hurried into the kitchen, stopping in front of the broom closet, where his treats were kept. Pendleton had proved over and over that he knew some words—*outside, walk, come, no,* and *bad,* for example—but *treat* was the word he knew best. I took a box of biscuits, giant size, from the cupboard, and rattled it in front of his face. Now he was mine. I stuck a biscuit, just one, in my jacket pocket, collected a baggie and the scooper. He trotted after me to the door—his trot was clumsy and shambling, with a lot of side-to-side motion—down the stairs to the outside door and onto the street.

"Where to?" I said. We could go up the hill toward Monsieur Señor's or down past a long line of brownstones with a tree in front of every second one, trees which interested all the neighborhood dogs except Pendleton. He chose neither, instead ramming his snout against the pocket with the biscuit inside.

"First you have to perform," I told him. He gazed at me for one of those long, still moments of his. I jiggled the leash, hoping to break the spell. He did some more gazing, then turned right and headed down the hill. That was his usual choice, but I could see he regretted it almost at once, because coming the other way was another dog, a very small dog being walked by a very small old lady. Pendleton backed up and cowered against me, almost knocking me down. The very small dog yipped at Pendleton as it went by; the old lady had a grim smile on her face. I jerked on the leash and got Pendleton restarted.

"What's your problem?" I said. Pendleton was a shelter dog, but we'd had him for almost two years now, two years of living like a prince. "Wag your tail. Show some spirit." His tail, a strange little stub, remained in the hanging-down position.

We walked down the block, Pendleton ignoring every tree. The wind rose. I glanced up at the night sky, saw no moon or stars, just the dirty pink city glow. We went by the vacant lot with the fence that always had a big hole even though it got repaired all the time—

Pendleton slowing down but not quite stopping—and came to Vincero, a fancy restaurant on the corner. A limo idled outside. And what was this? A guy wrapped in a blanket sat on the sidewalk, a paper cup in his gnarled hand. There seemed to be more street people around these days. I started getting tense, not sure why.

Pendleton shifted onto the street, getting as far as possible from the guy in the blanket. I was tugging at the leash when Vincero's door opened and a fat man came out, laughing and buttoning his leather coat. The driver jumped out of the limo and opened the rear door. The fat man moved toward the limo. He stepped in front of the guy in the blanket.

The guy in the blanket said, "Sir? A little help here?"

The fat man paused and stared down at the guy in the blanket. "Three simple words," he said. "Get. A. Job." Then he turned toward the limo, the lights from the Vincero sign gleaming on his heavy gold watch.

I felt the silver heart flutter on my wrist. And then: *wham.* The pressure ball in my skull awoke just like that, but far more powerful than before, and passing through its stages much faster. First the pain—but there and gone so quickly I wasn't sure I'd even felt it—and the electric currents to my eyes, this time somehow knocking my glasses right off my face. Then, flashing from my eyes— my vision suddenly perfect—came that red-gold beam, now hot: I heard the air sizzle. The beam struck the fat man's heavy gold watch as he got into the limo, and then faded in an instant. The limo drove off.

My vision went back to fuzzy right away. I bent down, found my glasses, unbroken in the gutter, and put them on. That was when I spotted the gold watch, lying just a few feet away. Whoa! What exactly had just happened? Beam or no beam? If beam, how was it possible no one else had noticed? And if no beam, what was the story with the watch? Now I was scared a bit, but of what I wasn't sure, and was still bent down in the gutter, kind of stunned, when the guy in the blanket brushed past me, scooped up the gold watch, scuttled through the hole in the fence, and vanished in the shadows of the vacant lot.

Dad came home about an hour after I got back from walking Pendleton. I could smell the take-out from Your Thai even before he opened the door. I was starving.

"You must be starving," Dad said, as we sat down at the kitchen table.

"I'm okay," I said.

Dad poured himself a glass of wine, swirled it around, and sipped. I opened the cartons. Yes: *kaeng phet ped yang,* my addiction. Red curry with roast duck, the look, the smell, the taste, all amazing. Plus I liked saying the Thai words even though I didn't even know which one was *duck.* We ate with chopsticks, Dad and I, handling them no problem; we were good with chopsticks in this family, excluding Nonna, of course.

"Dad?" I said, after I'd cleaned my plate twice. "Remember what you were saying about the imagination playing tricks?"

"When was this?" He refilled his glass.

"I don't know—a while back. When you were talking about memoirs and stuff."

"Sure," he said. "The imagination and memory. They bump up against each other, intersect, crisscross like . . ." He reached around for a pencil on the counter, made a quick note on one of Your Thai's paper napkins.

"Well, um, does your imagination play tricks on you?" I said.

"In the sense of undermining the concept of objective reality, you mean?"

Objective reality? That was what, again? "More, like, maybe making things happen."

Dad swirled the wine around some more, took another sip. "The imagination makes everything happen," he said, "at least in my work."

"Yeah," I said. "But I mean, like, in the real world."

Dad's eyebrows rose. "You don't think writers operate in the real world?"

"Of course they do, Dad." Although it wasn't actually something I'd ever thought about, and sounding so sure didn't feel right. At the same time, going the other way, a way that led to my dad maybe not being part of the real world, didn't feel right either.

"And, Robbie?" he added. "Don't take this personally, and it's not a big deal, but you're getting into that 'like' habit again."

I felt myself turning red, always hated when that happened. I rose and started cleaning up. The "like" habit—so what? "When's Mom coming home?" I said, over at the sink, my back to Dad.

Dad poured more wine, texting at the same time. A slight pause and then: "Not for an hour at least. She's really getting slammed these days."

I went into the living room, a cool space with a highly polished hardwood floor and gleaming steel furniture that wasn't as uncomfortable as you might think; and cooled down. I flicked on the TV and went back and forth through the channels. Friday night. After a while, I felt like calling a friend, but I was between friends at that point, as I mentioned earlier. One of my best friends at Joe Louis was Inez Marcos. I'd bumped into her on the F train over Thanksgiving, and she'd said to call her and maybe we'd do something, and I had, once or twice, leaving messages in her voice mail. Now I tried her again. Why not?

Beep. "The number you have dialed is no longer in service." I zipped through the channels one more time, suddenly feeling wiped out.

"I'm going to bed."

"Night," Dad called from the kitchen.

"Night," I called back.

I fell asleep real quick, not like me at all. In my dreams (and maybe I should leave this out, on account of this old saying my dad told me about: describe a dream, lose a reader), I was soaring over Manhattan. I'd heard about soaring dreams—overheard about them, actually, from this conversation an older Thatcher girl was having with her friends, all about her shrink—but never had one before. Strange that I'd be conscious of that and dreaming the dream at the same time. Anything as powerful as dreams had to be important, right? So what was wrong with describing them?

"Hey, sleepyhead."

I opened my eyes, and there was Mom, gazing down, full morning light streaming in from the window.

"Hi, Mom." Her face looked soft and tired. Mom was an associate at a big law firm in Manhattan. She'd billed 2,400 hours last year, but there was plenty of work time that didn't get billed, so you probably had to add another 1,000 hours or so on top of that, making 3,400. Divide that by forty-nine, because Mom got three weeks off, although she'd only been able to take ten days last year, and you come up with a pretty tiring number. Also *associate* meant you were a real lawyer but not a partner. Partners were the big time, made way more money, but not all the associates got to be partners, in fact just a few every year. That was one of Mom's main worries.

"Are you feeling all right?" she said.

"Yeah."

"You look a little flushed." She put her hand on my forehead. Mom had a real gentle touch. "You don't feel hot. Everything okay?"

"Yeah." Which was when the strange events, or imaginings, of yesterday came back to me. Or could it all have been part of my dream? "I had one of those soaring dreams," I said.

"I used to have them all the time—I forget what they're supposed to mean," Mom said. "Chas will know. Remind me to ask him when he wakes up." She checked her watch. "Time to go if we're going. But if you don't feel up to it—"

"I'm fine."

I got up, brushed my teeth, and splashed water on my face, the tiny silver heart flashing in the mirror. How quickly my wrist had adapted to the bracelet; I really didn't even feel it. I threw on some clothes, put my hair in a ponytail, and five minutes later we were on the street, my mom, Pendleton, and I. Saturday mornings— if Mom wasn't called in to work, in which case I went by myself—we volunteered at a soup kitchen called Bread not far from Joe Louis. Another sunny day, maybe colder than yesterday. I blew out a little puff of air, saw my breath. Mom held Pendleton's leash, hooked her other arm through mine. She had her hair in a ponytail, too, and wore her Mets cap. I got in a very good mood.

"We beat Welland yesterday."

"Did you? That's great. How's that coach, Ms. . . ."

"Kleinberg. She's got the sweetest shot you ever saw."

Mom glanced at me—we were almost eye-to-eye now, with the way I was growing—and laughed. "I'm guessing things are getting better at Thatcher?" she said. "You're more comfortable now?"

Not really, but I didn't want to darken this nice morning in any way, so I said, "Yeah, some."

Mom gave my arm a squeeze. Pendleton raised his leg next to a parked motorcycle. Mom dragged him away. He looked kind of ridiculous—one leg up, trailing a yellow stream—but had a dignified expression on his face at the same time, and Mom and I both started laughing.

"I'm loving this," Mom said. "Out of the office! Yes!" She took a deep breath.

"Did Nonna ever work, Mom?"

Mom shook her head. "Things were different in those days," she said. "My dad—your grandfather—did well. And then when he died, he left behind a very good insurance policy."

I'd never known my mom's dad—he'd died years before I was born.

We walked in silence for a while. Saturday mornings

there were always lots of people on the street. They say real New Yorkers never make eye contact, and maybe that's true, but most all of them are real good at snatching quick glances at the faces going by, including me. That's one of the very best things about the city: all those different faces.

Mom said, "I know what you're thinking: do Dad and I have insurance policies?"

"Actually, not," I said.

"No?"

"I was thinking, What did he die of, your father?"

"I'm sure I've told you."

"You just said he got very sick. What kind of sick?"

"He had a brain tumor," my mom said.

"Oh," I said. I looked at Mom. Her eyes were a little misty. She smiled at me. "He'd have been so—" Whatever that thought was, Mom didn't finish it, because at that moment Pendleton spotted a cat in a window and backed up abruptly, almost knocking us down.

"As for insurance," Mom said, after we'd gotten untangled from the leash and were on our way again, "the answer is no. It's hard to get your dad to talk about that kind of thing."

"Because he's an artist, right, Mom?"

"I guess," Mom said.

"What's this memoir all about, anyway?"

"Hard to say. He's still in the mulling-it-over stage." She was a big believer in Dad's talent.

Bread was halfway down the next block—I could already see people outside. Mom and I had been volunteering there for a year or so. She worked in the kitchen, and I helped serve food to the people in the line. There was always hot soup—chicken noodle went over best— plus a pasta dish like spaghetti or linguini or sometimes lasagna, plus sandwiches, chips, cookies, soda, coffee, and tea. Lots of the same people turned up every Saturday. Sometimes after I'd filled their bowls or handed over a sandwich, they said "bless you, angel," which bothered me, or just "thanks" or "*gracias*," which were fine, or nothing at all, which was what I preferred, hard to say why. My favorite customer—that was what we were supposed to call them—was this old guy called Little Zane. He wasn't little at all, but kind of huge, and always had a harmonica in his pocket, which he sometimes played after he'd finished eating. Little Zane was amazing on the harmonica; the word was that he'd played in the Village with Bob Dylan when Dylan was just starting out, but if he had, he never talked about it. He mostly just said the titles of the songs after he played, like "Black Snake Moan" or "You Got to Move."

"Big crowd today," Mom said, and as we got closer, we saw they weren't lined up but were sort of milling around. We moved through them to the front door. Bread was in a storefront in an old brick building and had big windows, which made it easy to see that it was dark and empty inside.

A sign was pasted on the door. "Hey," I said. "What's going on?" The sign read SORRY—CLOSED UNTIL FURTHER NOTICE. "Mom?"

My mom squeezed in beside me—Pendleton whimpering, maybe because of all the people—and checked the sign. "I have no idea," she said.

Somewhere in the crowd a woman yelled, "Nothing changes, brothers and sisters, nothing changes." After that came a short period of muttering and shuffling around and then all the customers sort of melted away. I spotted Little Zane headed toward the subway entrance, his head down. And wait! Who was that, just behind him, a jacketless kid with dreads, wearing just a long-sleeve tee? Tut-Tut? Sure looked like him. Had Tut-Tut been in the crowd at Bread? Was he hungry? He disappeared from view, either down into the subway or around the corner.

Mom and I stood by the door, Pendleton panting beside us. I put my face to the glass. Way in the dimness at the back, I saw movement.

"Someone's in there," I said.

Mom gazed peered through the window. "It's Claire."

Claire was a nun—but one of those nuns who didn't wear the nun costume, so she didn't seem scary—and also she was the main person in charge of Bread. Mom rapped on the glass. Claire emerged from the shadows, glanced up and down the street, then opened the door.

"Hello, Jane," she said. "Hi, Robbie." Her eyes had dark patches under them, and her face looked ashy. "Sorry you came for nothing," she said. "There was just no time to notify everybody, and right up until this morning, I thought we'd work something out."

"I don't understand," my mom said. "What's going on?"

"There's a new landlord," Claire said. "Some developer, apparently. He wants us out."

"He can't just do that," my mom said. "There's a whole process—it can take a year or more."

"But he can raise the rent," Claire said. "In fact, he doubled it. And with the funding cuts, there's no way. He slapped a lien on us yesterday and somehow cut off all our suppliers."

"How did he do that?"

"I don't know."

"What's the new rent?"

"Eight thousand a month."

"My God," my mom said. That was the only part of the conversation I actually grasped: eight thousand dollars.

"And our cash on hand at the moment is fifty-three hundred," Claire said. She produced a clipboard. "We're gathering a petition to send to the developer—with copies to City Hall and the governor's office."

"We'll sign," said Mom.

Claire handed me the clipboard. There were signatures almost to the bottom of the top page. I signed my name—R. M. Forester, which was how I'd been signing my name lately, the *M* standing for Matilda, a total blunder of a choice on my parents' part—and handed the clipboard to my mom.

She read the writing at the top of the page, what the petition actually said, I supposed, a step I'd skipped. All of a sudden, she paused and her mouth opened slightly. "I'm afraid I can't sign this," she said.

"No?" said Claire, her eyebrows rising in surprise.

"It's a conflict of interest," Mom said.

"I don't understand," said Claire. Neither did I.

"With my work," Mom said.

Claire stepped back, like she'd been shocked. "You worked on taking over this building and raising the rent?" she said.

Mom shook her head, hard and quick, as if shaking off the very idea. "I know nothing about this specifically—debt is my area. But the name of the landlord"—Mom pointed with the pen—"NBRP? That stands for the

New Brooklyn Redevelopment Project, meaning that what happened here is connected to what I do."

"The New Brooklyn Redevelopment Project," said Claire. "Is that the one being pushed by the Sheldon Gunn Organization?"

"He's one of our biggest clients," Mom said.

4

There wasn't much conversation after that, probably a good thing because it got kind of awkward. Soon Claire locked the door and went away. Mom took a deep breath. That was something she did deliberately from time to time. Sometimes she'd even speak out loud: "Deep breath, Janie." No one called her Janie but her. This wasn't one of those times; instead she said, "How about a muffin?"

"Okay."

We crossed the street to one of those little hole-in-the-wall places that didn't even have a name, but we knew from experience that the muffins were good. There were three rickety tables inside, all unoccupied. We sat at the least rickety and ordered muffins—cranberry for me, blueberry and acai for mom—and tea. Tea was Mom's drink. She picked at her muffin, sipped her tea, gazing across the street at the darkened windows of Bread. Long walks, or even not-so-long ones, tended to tire Pendleton out; he fell asleep under the table right away.

"You work for the guy who closed us down, Mom?" I said. "Is that what happened?"

She put down her mug, a tiny wavelet of tea spilling over the edge. "I work for Jaggers and Tulkinghorn." That was the name of Mom's firm. From the boardwalk on the Heights, where we sometimes took Pendleton on an outing, you could look across the river and see her building in Lower Manhattan, one of those enormous towers. Mom's office was on the second floor from the top, and she would have had a view of the Statue of Liberty, but a taller building stood in between. "The Sheldon Gunn Organization is a client. One of many."

"What's he like?"

"Who?"

"Sheldon Gunn."

Mom laughed, not a happy kind of laugh, more sharp and quickly cut off. "I've never met him. It doesn't work that way."

"He calls you on the phone?"

Mom shook her head. "I don't deal with him at all. My contact is an in-house lawyer, and it's mostly done through e-mails."

"What's 'it'?"

"My work? Structuring debt—haven't we been through this?"

"Let's go through it again," I said.

Mom went through it again. There were oceans of debt out there, which was just the flip side of lending . . . or something like that, and then I lost the thread. "The pressure," she said, reaching the end, "comes from the deadlines and the fact that you just can't make a mistake." I was sure of only one thing: Dad's job was better than Mom's.

"So, uh, why does Sheldon Gunn want to wreck Bread?" I asked.

"It's not really a question of that," Mom said. "He's probably never heard of Bread."

"But he must know about all these people who come to get a meal."

"Maybe," Mom said. "In general."

"Then couldn't you could call him and, you know, fill him in?"

Mom gave me a long look, like she was sizing me up, kind of strange, since we were mother and daughter.

"That would certainly clear up any doubt about whether I'm on the partner track or not," she said, which blew by me, but there was no time for a follow-up because at that moment Mom got a text. She checked it and sighed.

"You have to go in today?"

She nodded, downed the rest of her tea.

"To work for Sheldon Gunn?"

My mom isn't one of those people who gets annoyed very often, so when she does, it's always a surprise. "I told you—" She stopped herself, took a deep breath, and her voice went back to normal. "No," she said, "this is something else." Mom rose. I wrapped the rest of my muffin in my napkin and stuck it in my pocket for later. We woke Pendleton and went outside. At the same time, two big black cars drove up and parked in front of Bread.

A man got out of each one. They were both rich looking in that well-dressed Manhattan way, the collars of their dark topcoats turned up.

"Oh, my God," Mom said, and just as she said it, the shorter of the men glanced across the street and saw her.

"Jane?" he called. His gaze went to me, then to Pendleton, then back to my mom. "Did you get called on this?"

"No, I—" Mom began, but then the short man—bald with a round face and small features kind of lost in it—waved her over in an impatient sort of way. Mom hesitated. I thought maybe she was thinking of handing me the leash and telling me to wait where I was, but that didn't happen and the next thing I knew, we were crossing the street, Pendleton hanging back the way he did if meeting new people was a possibility, but not actually digging in his heels.

"Mom? What—"

"Jane?" the short man said. "Did Mark send you? I don't understand."

"No," Mom said. "I—"

"Andrew?" the taller man interrupted. "What's going on?"

Andrew, the shorter man—he also had a thick neck and very broad shoulders—said, "I'm finding that out. This is one of our associates, but she works in debt, not real estate, so I'm a little puzzled—"

The taller man held his hand out to Mom. "Sheldon Gunn," he said. "Pleased to meet you."

Sheldon Gunn! I thought of that phrase "speak of the devil," but Sheldon Gunn didn't look at all like a devil. He had swept-back silvery hair, smooth skin, and a handsome face, reminding me of one of those top-hatted actors in old black-and-white movies.

Mom shook hands with Sheldon Gunn. "Jane Forester," she said. "And there's no puzzle. We . . . we were just out for a walk. This is my daughter, Robbie."

"Um," I said, forgetting to extend my hand, not doing a good job on the whole introduction thing in general, but I was distracted by what my mom had just said, since we weren't just out for a walk.

"Hello there," said Sheldon Gunn, giving me a smile.

"Um," I said again. His smile vanished in a flash, and his eyes changed, too, like he'd stopped seeing me. How dumb could I be? I got mad at myself for being such a useless dweeb, and in my madness blurted out the first thing that came to mind. "What about Bread?"

"Bread?" said Sheldon Gunn.

"Just one of the former tenants, I believe," said Andrew. "Not important. Nice running into you, Jane."

"And you," said my mom, turning to go and giving Pendleton's leash a little tug.

Meanwhile Andrew was unrolling a big set of plans. "Now, what I wanted to show you, Sheldon, is this suggestion of the planners, that the parking garage could come all the way to here and replace this whole block, so that . . ." Sheldon Gunn bent his head to examine the plans, but I stopped being aware of what was happening out in the world, because inside my head the pressure was suddenly building, faster than ever before, all the stages speeding by—electric ball, vision, pain, fluttering heart—and the red-gold beam flashed out, aimed hip level at Sheldon Gunn's side. Then something fell from under the folds of Gunn's topcoat and landed on the sidewalk with a very soft thud. It took a strange long sideways bounce in my direction and landed at my feet. Without a thought, like a figure in a dream, maybe of the soaring kind, I stepped on whatever had fallen and then, after making sure that no one was looking, I picked it up and dropped it in my pocket. By now I knew what

I had in there: a fat wad of bills, neatly packed as though they'd just come from the bank, Benjamin Franklin on top. And that without-a-thought part wasn't quite true.

I glanced around. Andrew and Sheldon Gunn were examining the plans, their backs to me. Pendleton had gotten his leash twisted around a parking meter, and my mom was trying to free him. No one had seen a thing. As for the red-gold beam, I was starting to get used to its invisibility to everyone but me.

"Come on, Robbie," Mom said. "Let's get going."

All the way home I could feel that wad in my pocket. Or was it just the muffin I was feeling? I wanted desperately to make sure, especially about the Benjamin Franklin part—oh, the imagination and how it plays tricks, from out of nowhere a big concept in my life—but I didn't.

"Are you all right?" Mom said, glancing at me. "You look a little flushed."

"I'm fine." Oh, yeah? Getting used to the appearance of a red-gold beam visible only to yourself was fine? Comfortable with being—let's face it—kind of a thief? Was I going crazy?

"And your voice sounds funny."

"Funny how?"

"Like you're upset about something."

"Well, of course, Mom. Bread. Aren't you upset, too?"

Mom nodded. She opened her mouth to say something, but then came a vibration on her phone and another text arrived.

When we got home there was a note from Dad on the fridge: "Gone trolling." That was his expression for taking a long walk, hoping to hook some ideas. Mom started packing her briefcase for the office. I went upstairs.

Maybe I should describe my room. It's small, just big enough for my bed, desk, and chest of drawers, but in the city you're lucky to have a bedroom all to yourself. The walls are decorated with pictures of volcanoes: Vesuvius, St. Helen's, Mauna Loa, Etna, Santorini, Nyiragongo (my favorite because I like the name). I did a project on volcanoes in fifth grade, and the pictures have been up there ever since. There's also a window that looks out on the back of other buildings like ours and a tiny garden down below. Sometimes in warm weather I climb out and sit on the fire escape, actually a no-no from my parents' point of view, but it's perfectly safe. What else? Oh, yeah, Pookie's tail hanging from the bedpost. I'd had a stuffed dog named Pookie until one day I was at school and Pendleton got hold of him.

I took off my jacket, emptied my pocket. Not my imagination: in my hand, covered with muffin crumbs, I held a thick wad of bills, Benjamin Franklin on top. I started counting. One, two, three, four, five—all of them Benjamins! I kept going—seventeen, eighteen, nineteen, Benjamins each and every one, my hands no longer steady. In the end I counted thirty-one. Thirty-one hundred dollars! Also, thirty-one was a number that had meaning in my life: it was on my basketball jersey. Okay, maybe not a lot of meaning—especially since the number I'd wanted was six, already worn by Ashanti—but some, and I took it as a good sign, encouragement for this plan that had been forming in my head the whole time.

First I had to re-count the money, just to make sure. One, two, three, four, five—

There was a knock on the door. Mom's knock. I hadn't even heard her footsteps. Did my hearing suck, too? Was I wandering the world with practically no senses at all? And had I been counting aloud?

"Robbie?"

The door opened. By that time I was sitting on the bed, bills and muffin underneath me. "Yeah?"

Mom looked in. She'd changed her jacket for her coat. "I'll only be two or three hours," she said. "Hopefully."

"Okay."

"What are you going to do?"

"Do?"

"While I'm gone. How about calling that Ashanti kid? Doesn't she live close by?"

"I don't really know her."

"You could get to know her."

"Mom. She's in eighth grade. Don't worry about me. I'll be fine."

"Sure?"

"Yeah. Uh, Mom?"

"Yes?"

"Who's Andrew, exactly?"

"A senior partner."

"What's he like?"

"A shark."

I laughed.

"The kind," Mom went on, "that has to keep swimming or it drowns, so they're always hungry."

I stopped laughing.

Mom left. As soon as I heard the door close downstairs, I counted the money again. And once more. By that time I was forming opinions on what Ben Franklin must have been like, just from seeing his face so much. But that wasn't the point. The point was I had in my hands $3,100. I cleaned up the remains of the muffin.

5

The house grew quiet, at least quiet for the city, meaning a constant noisy hum with no nearby sirens, shouting, sudden braking, garbage trucks, or low-flying airplanes. Real actual quiet, which I'd experienced at times, such as last summer when I spent two weeks at a camp in Vermont, bothered me. I got up, stuffed the money back in my jacket pocket, and started for the door. At that point, I got the idea of wearing my hoodie instead of the jacket, hard to say why. My hoodie—a heavy sweatshirt with a hand-warmer pocket and the Mets NY logo on the chest—hung in the closet. I opened it and heard the voice of Mitch the landlord rising from his apartment down below. This was a strange quirk of my closet, something to do with the pipes, my dad said. Sometimes I could even make out the words, like now, for instance: "A quarter point?" Mitch was saying, maybe on the phone. "Why would I bother?" Was he talking about money? A big difference between adults and kids occurred to me then: adults talked an awful lot about money, and kids did not.

But at the moment I was a kid with money on my mind. I put on my hoodie, transferred the $3,100 to the hand-warmer pocket, and went downstairs. Pendleton lay under the table, eyes open but not moving, in one of those trancelike states of his. There were all kinds of rules about going out by myself, such as never at night, only certain streets allowed, and having a good reason, which included meeting friends or shopping for a necessity we were out of, such as kibble; plus always calling Mom or Dad first, and failing that, leaving a note on the fridge. I left a note, right beside my dad's: "Back in a flash."

Not long after that, I was standing in front of the no-name hole-in-the-wall café again, looking across the street at Bread. It wasn't a busy street for cars, and not many walkers were around either, maybe because the sky had turned cloudy and a cold wind had risen. The windows of Bread were dark, and I saw no sign of anyone inside. So things were going my way! Then I thought of something Ms. Kleinberg liked to say: You make your own luck. Suddenly I was in a great mood, like I could accomplish just about anything. I looked both ways and crossed the street, pulling on my hood at the same time. Why did I do that? I didn't have anything bad in mind, quite the opposite.

The sign was still on the door at Bread: SORRY—CLOSED UNTIL FURTHER NOTICE. Someone had tagged the front window, a tag I'd never seen before that said *vudu* in thick purple letters. First tag I'd ever seen on Bread; even though I had nothing against tags, I couldn't help thinking how fast things could fall apart. Graffiti showing up almost right away: what was next? Floods and fires, like one of those disaster movies about the city? But none of that changed my mood. Wasn't I trying to keep things from falling apart? I walked right up to the door, a door with a slot for letters, and looked both ways again. A woman entering the café, a man hailing a cab, a couple hurrying toward the bus stop at the next corner, none of them watching me. I bent toward the door, took the wad of money from my hand-warming pocket, and—thinking too late that an envelope or even a rubber band might have been nice—shoved $3,100 inside. The bills landed with a faint fluttering sound.

I backed away, glanced around again—out of nowhere, someone was standing on the sidewalk, practically within touching distance! My heart started pounding in my chest so hard I thought I might rise straight up in the air. And then I saw the face of this person, a small person with a face not easy to see, on account of he, too, was wearing a hoodie.

Tut-Tut.

"Oh, my God," I said. "You scared me to death."

"S-s-s-s-," said Tut-Tut. "S-s-s-s—"

We stood there. I saw that Tut-Tut had very nice eyes: the shape of them, the color, and this impression of depth. Also, he was shivering a bit, his lips ashy from cold. His hoodie was of the thin kind, and he wore flip-flops way past the season for flip-flops; his jeans were torn, but not in a cool way.

"Do you live near here?" I said. "Did I see you this morning?"

Tut-Tut didn't answer. He went to the door, peered through the glass. I looked in, too. Dark inside, but not so dark you couldn't see the money scattered on the floor. Had Tut-Tut caught me pushing it through the slot?

"Tut-Tut?" I said. He turned to me. "This is not what . . ." That feeble try ran out of gas. This is not what it looks like? Such as what? A robbery in reverse? Meanwhile Tut-Tut was staring at me with those eyes of his. "What?" I said. "What?"

"B-b-," he said. "B-b-b-b—" He pointed through the glass. "M-m-," he said. "M-m-m—"

"I know," I said. "It's kind of complicated. I don't want you to—"

At that moment came a cry from across the street. "Hey! Is that my man Tut-Tut?"

I turned, saw three boys on skateboards, all bigger

than me and Tut-Tut. They glided quickly over, clattered up onto the sidewalk.

"Hey, Tut-Tut, my man, wha's up?" said the biggest. I recognized him from Joe Louis, a rough kid a year or two ahead of me, the kind of kid who scared the parents of kids like me into forking out all that money for private school. "Tell us a story, little man Tut-Tut."

"Yeah," said another. "Like how come you don't have no green card."

"I-I-," said Tut-Tut, "I-I-I—"

"I-I-I-," the rough kids said. "I-I-I-I-I-ay-ay-sombrero." Then they circled around us on their boards, laughing and starting up on "G-g-g-g-green c-c-c-c-card," and stuff like that.

I said, "Leave him alone."

They all turned on me. "Who's this geek?" said the biggest one.

"Why don't you guys just move on?" I said, but don't make the mistake of thinking I sounded tough: my voice was real shaky.

"Why don't you guys just move on?" the big one said, mimicking me and making a limp-wristed move.

Then one of the others reached out and flicked my hoodie back off my face. "It's one of those rich kids," he said.

And the third one snatched my glasses and held them

just out of reach. No glasses, so of course my vision got blurry.

"We'll let you buy 'em back," said the biggest one. "How much you got on you, rich kid?"

"I'm not a rich kid," I said, pretty close to crying. "Give me my glasses."

"Four-eyes rich kid wants her glasses," said the kid who had them, tossing them in the air and almost not catching them.

"St-st-st-," said Tut-Tut.

"St-st-st-st-st-," went all three guys, spit flying from their mouths.

This was bad, and I had no idea how to keep it from getting worse, but then came some surprises. First, Tut-Tut stepped up, getting in between me and that biggest guy. Of course the biggest guy had no fear of Tut-Tut, grabbing him by the front of his hoodie.

"St-st-st-," said Tut-Tut.

At that moment the whole electric ball thing sprang to life in my head, the pressure getting real intense, the pain very bad, but no force lines or whatever they were connecting to my eyes, although my vision got better at once. The biggest guy shoved Tut-Tut aside like nothing, and he would have fallen except that he bumped into me and I caught him. And as I held his skinny chest, I felt those force lines, not moving toward my eyes this time but down my arms like Tasers or something, so powerful, sparking hot off my fingertips and jolting Tut-Tut's chest.

"Ow," he cried out in pain; at the same time, my own pain was gone, utterly.

"What's with you, you little wimp?" said the biggest guy. "I barely touched you."

Tut-Tut straightened. He faced these mean kids. So brave! But he was going to get the crap beat out of him, and probably me, too. Then Tut-Tut opened his mouth, and I got the biggest shock of my life. Tut-Tut spoke, and he spoke in a strong, clear, commanding voice.

"Give back her glasses," he said, no stuttering, no pausing, no struggle; he had a slight accent, kind of French. "And then," he went on, "get out of here."

Dead silence. The three rough kids all gazed at Tut-Tut, astonishment on their faces. The kid with my glasses handed them back to me, his movements slow, like he was hypnotized. Then he and the third kid backed away; only the big one stayed where he was. "You could talk all this time? You're playing a big joke on everybody?"

Tut-Tut took a step toward him. He was much smaller than the big kid, but it didn't seem that way. "I have a knife," Tut-Tut said, in this new voice of his, "and I know how to use it."

Zoom. All three of them bolted, not even taking

their boards. We watched them till they rounded a corner and vanished from sight.

Tut-Tut turned to me.

"I'm scared," he said. He started shaking.

"Why?" I said. But I was scared too. Maybe Tut-Tut knew the reason. I sure didn't.

"Because I can talk," he said. He shook more and more. "What's going on? I've never talked in my whole life. Except inside my head, only now it's getting outside, too."

"Well," I said, "that's good." Maybe my lamest remark ever.

"And when you caught me just now?"

"Yeah?"

"When your hands were on my chest?"

"Yeah?"

"I felt a jolt. It went right through my body." Tears ran down his face.

"And then you could talk?"

"Yeah," Tut-Tut said. More tears, and suddenly his face was shining. The shaking stopped and Tut-Tut raised his hands to the sky. "I can talk," he cried. "I'd stopped thinking this could ever happen. I can talk! I'm talking!" He looked at me, his eyes so bright. "You know what's funny?" he said.

"What?"

"I don't know what to say."

He started laughing. I laughed, too. Then we were hugging. I could feel the bones of Tut-Tut's spine and all the ribs under the skin of his back.

"I can talk," he said. We let go of each other, stepped back a bit. "Listen to me," Tut-Tut said. "I'm speaking English! Also I can speak Creole." And he spoke something in a foreign language that sounded a little like French. He laughed again, then clasped his chest and spun in a circle. "I can ask questions," he said.

That had to be amazing. "What's the first one?" I said.

"What's your name?" he said.

"Robbie. What's yours?"

"Tut-Tut."

"I mean your real name."

"Toussaint."

"Cool. I'll call you Toussaint."

He shook his head. "Tut-Tut's better. It's my nickname, my American nickname." He glanced through the door, down onto the floor of Bread where the money lay. "So did I see what I thought I saw?" he said.

"I can explain," I said. But could I? Where to begin? The basketball game, or cut right to Sheldon Gunn's $3,100? And while I was trying to line things up in some sort of order, my vision, still in that hawklike phase that always accompanied these—fits? Was that the word? I shied away from it. But the point was my vision was deteriorating back to normal again, all the fine details of Tut-Tut's face growing less fine. "Bread has to close up because they can't make rent. Some money . . . fell into my hands, and—"

"Yeah?" he said. "Like how?"

"Well," I said, my vision getting blurrier, "something really strange has been happening to me." I put on my glasses.

"Yeah?" said Tut-Tut. "Like wha-wh-wh-wh-wh-w-w-w-w . . ."

"Tut-Tut?"

His eyes, his mouth, all opening wide: the look people get when they're about to get mowed down or blown away by something terrible, like an earthquake or a hurricane. "I-," he said. He tried so hard, on and on, veins popping out in his neck, his face swelling up. "I-I-I-I-I-I-I-I-I-" But it was no good. Tut-Tut put his hands over his ears and screamed, a long unstuttering sound, but not speech.

"Tut-Tut!" I reached out to him. "What's happening? Try to get back to how you were feeling when—"

But before I could even finish with whatever dumb notion that was going to be, Tut-Tut had wheeled away and taken off. He ran right out of his flip-flops, and something fell from his pocket. Tut-Tut was very fast, the fastest kid I'd ever seen. I'm a pretty good runner, too, but catching him was out of the question. All I could do was pick up the flip-flops and the thing that had fallen from his pocket, which turned out to be a can of purple spray paint.

I took a long detour on the way home. I've always liked walking, but that didn't explain this particular walk, which led me past the subway stop a block and a half from school; it was more that my feet simply wanted to go in that direction.

What I was hoping for was to see the old homeless woman back in her usual spot and return the bracelet, but she wasn't there. I went into the newsstand and up to the counter. The man behind it was busy with a Sudoku puzzle. He glanced up.

"Hi," I said. "Um, the old woman? Who sits out front all the time? I was wondering whether . . ."

"She died," the man said, and went back to his puzzle.

My knees got weak; it turned out not to be just an expression. I felt a train rumbling down below.

After that came the illness part. I remember walking home with the flip-flops and the spray paint; I remember seeing that neither Mom nor Dad was back yet; I remember feeling way too hot, and also way too tall, which was very weird, plus, everything looked yellow at the edges, like old newspapers. Then I was in my bed, and hotter than ever, and Pendleton was beside me, licking my face from time to time. His tongue felt nice and cool.

Time passed, maybe not a lot. When you're sick, time loses its strict shape, starts ballooning and/or shrinking, like an image in a funhouse mirror. Mom and Dad appeared, standing over me. My temperature got taken—I didn't like the feel of that glass stick under my tongue; worried looks got exchanged; headaches were mentioned. Did I have one? No, but I'd had a few lately. The worried looks grew more worried, as though the guy who painted that *Scream* picture was doing their portraits.

Whispers went back and forth:

"Headaches? Didn't your father . . ."

"Chas, must you always jump to the most . . ."

Whispers buzzing around like insects, but not as loud, more like insects with mufflers. That phrase "insects with mufflers" went round and round my brain, round and round my brain, and wouldn't stop. A strange idea hit me—that I now understood stuttering from the inside—and vanished almost right away. Insects with mufflers, insects with mufflers.

Then there were phone calls. "One-oh-four-point-five." And a taxi ride across the Brooklyn Bridge, with me lying back and the whole structure, all those beams and arches, lit up against the night sky, a scary image for some reason; and walking into the hospital, although Mom and Dad were kind of holding me up; and there was my uncle Joe, wearing a white coat and with a stethoscope around his neck. Uncle Joe—my dad's older brother—was a surgeon at the hospital.

"Hey, cutie," he said to me, laying his hand, so nice and cool, on my forehead. He looked like my dad except shorter-haired, heavier, and a lot older, although the difference was less than two years. "How're you feeling?"

"Joe," said my dad, "she's got a fever of—"

Uncle Joe held up his hand. My dad went silent.

"How're you feeling, cutie?"

"Not perfect," I said.

Uncle Joe smiled. We didn't see Uncle Joe very often, pretty much just Thanksgiving and maybe for dinner at his house in Saddle Brook (which Dad called Saddle Poop), New Jersey.

"We'll soon see about that," he said.

Crazily enough, I started feeling a bit better at that exact moment. Out in the hall, Dad was talking in a low voice to some other doctor: ". . . my wife's father, so I was wondering about the possibility of a genetic—" The door closed.

"Let's talk about these headaches," said Uncle Joe. "When was the last time you saw the eye doctor?"

"Last summer," I said. "Just before school. Right eye minus three, left minus two-point-five."

Uncle Joe flashed a quick smile, looked a lot younger for a second or so. "And was that a change from the time before?"

"Yeah. I got new glasses."

"The ones you're wearing now?"

"Uh-huh."

"They look nice."

"Yeah? Thanks, Uncle Joe. The funny thing is when the headaches come, I don't need them."

"Oh?"

"Yeah. I can see just fine, but it doesn't last." And then there was the whole red–gold beam part. When was the time for bringing that up? Maybe it was all unreal, part of a fever dream. And what if something really bad was wrong with me? That five-letter word, starting with *T,* ending with *R*? I didn't even let my mind form it, although of course my mind kept trying and trying. Insects with mufflers, insects with mufflers. The next thing I knew, I was hotter again, and a nurse was feeding me ice chips. I remembered my dad once saying, "Joe's hopeless when it comes to that kind of thing."

"What are you hopeless at, Uncle Joe?"

"Did you say something, Robbie?"

Oops. Uncle Joe was gazing down at me; also we were on the move, me lying on a gurney, someone out of my field of vision pushing, and Uncle Joe walking alongside.

"Nothing to feel hopeless about," he said. "Have you bumped your head on anything lately? Taken a blow, playing sports, say?"

"Yes," I said. And then: "No."

Uncle Joe smiled. "Which is it?"

"No," I said. So weird. It was Ashanti who got hit in the head, but I really did feel like it was me.

"Sure?" he said.

"Um. Yeah."

We rounded a corner, came to a stop. Some tiles were missing from the ceiling, and the empty spaces up there looked endless and dark. I knew scary thoughts like that were just from the fever talking, but that didn't mean they went away.

"Know what an MRI is?" Uncle Joe said.

"Like an X-ray?"

"Yes," said Uncle Joe. "And even better for things like this. Up for it? It's noisy but completely painless."

Things like what? Did they have five letters, first one *T,* last one *R*? I kept that to myself. "Yeah, I'm up for it," I said.

"Got any metal on you?" he said, as we entered a room with a long white tube in the center.

"No."

"What about those earrings?"

"Oh, yeah."

I took off the earrings—my arms felt so heavy—and handed them to a woman in a white uniform.

"Anything else?" she said.

"No."

"What's that on your wrist? A friendship bracelet?"

I glanced down at it. "Yeah." Yes, a friendship bracelet, and of a very special kind.

"But that heart is metal, right?"

I handed over the bracelet and right away felt a bit strange without it, like I wasn't fully dressed.

They slid me into the tube. My job was to lie still. I lay still. Painless and noisy—like a giant was knocking hard at the outside of the tube—but somehow I fell asleep anyway. I was kind of an X-ray machine myself.

I woke up much later in a small dark room with Mom and Dad standing beside me.

Mom touched my hand. Her hand didn't feel cool. "How are you?" she said.

"Good." It was true. I felt way better.

"You were so brave in the MRI," she said.

Hey! You could be brave by falling asleep at the right moment. Maybe I could snooze my way to the Medal of Honor.

Uncle Joe and another doctor came in. "This is Dr. Ng," Uncle Joe said. "She's head of radiology."

It got very silent in the room. I could feel Mom and Dad tense up, and it really bothered me. I made a decision, years ahead of the game: when it was time for college, I was heading out of town.

Dr. Ng looked at me. "I'm happy to report," she said, "that the results were negative."

Negative? Oh, no, no, no. My heart started racing real fast, like it wanted to live, live, live.

False alarm. "Negative meaning good, right?" said my mom.

"Right," said Dr. Ng. "We found no evidence of disease or defect whatsoever. Robbie's brain is entirely normal."

So negative was good? My parents' eyes moistened. They each patted me, like I'd come up big.

"Can I go home now?" I said. "I feel fine."

Uncle Joe and Dr. Ng exchanged a glance. "Fever's down," said Uncle Joe. "Don't see why not."

"Joe," said my dad, "shouldn't we have a diagnosis?"

Uncle Joe gave him a quick look, kind of sharp. "Quite possibly a quick-acting virus. We can't say for sure."

"How would that explain the headaches?" Dad said.

"It wouldn't," said Uncle Joe. "No need for a connection. Lots of kids get headaches, often from stress."

"Stress?" said Dad, turning to me. "You haven't said anything about stress."

"Is it because of changing schools?" my mom asked me. "Didn't I tell you, Chas?"

Dr. Ng checked her pager. "Nice meeting you all." She left the room.

I just wanted out. I raised my voice. "There's no stress. I'm fine."

Uncle Joe checked his pager, too. "I'd suggest another

appointment with the ophthalmologist," he said. "And of course get in touch if anything . . . for any reason. Take care of yourself, Robbie." He handed over the plastic bag. "Here's your stuff."

"Thanks, Uncle Joe. Thanks for everything."

"Yes," said my mom. "Thanks, Joe."

"Yeah, thanks," said my dad.

"Don't mention it," said Uncle Joe.

In the taxi on the way home, I put on my earrings and slipped the bracelet back on my wrist. Ah. Dawn was breaking, a dark, drizzly, sunless dawn. It was beautiful.

My parents let me stay home on Monday. I didn't wake up till noon. Dad was down in the kitchen, working on his laptop.

"Hey, sleepyhead, how are you feeling?"

"Fine."

"Maybe I'll take Pendleton for his walk—he hasn't been out yet."

"Okay."

"Sure you'll be all right?"

"Dad. I'm fine."

He gazed at me. "You look okay," he said. "Kind of like . . ." His eyes shifted, drawn by some thought. It was possible I'd just been turned into a metaphor.

Dad took Pendleton for his walk. I really did feel fine—and starving. I poured a big bowl of cereal, sliced a banana, threw in some blueberries, and was just sitting down when the phone rang.

"Hello?"

"Robbie? It's Claire from Bread."

"Hi."

"Is your mom there?"

"She's at work."

"Well, I can tell you, since you're a volunteer, too. Please pass it on."

"Pass what on?"

Claire laughed, a giddy kind of laugh, which made her sound much younger and less nunlike—an unfair thought, but I had it anyway. "Good news. We're not closing down, at least not this month."

"Oh?"

"A benefactor has appeared on the scene. An anonymous benefactor, out of the blue. Or should I say by the grace of God?"

"Yeah?" I said. I preferred out of the blue; the implications of choice two were way too much.

"He simply shoved a whole wad of cash through the letter slot," Claire said.

He? That was interesting. First, it meant no one saw—except for Tut-Tut, of course. Second, why would

Claire assume the benefactor was a man? I didn't know, but it worked out nicely.

"Awesome," I said. "See you Saturday."

I went back to my cereal, got a perfect spoonful arranged with just the right balance of cereal, bananas, and blueberries, when the phone rang again. It was my mom.

"How are you feeling?"

"Fine."

"I've got a question for you."

"Yeah?" I put my spoon back in the bowl.

"Remember Sheldon Gunn—the man at Bread on Saturday?"

"Kinda."

"Did you see any suspicious characters around at the time?"

"Suspicious characters? Like how do you mean?"

"Andrew—the partner from the firm—told me Mr. Gunn seems to have had his pocket picked sometime on Saturday. He's pretty annoyed about it. Not because of the money so much."

"Because of what?"

"It's more of a pride thing. Apparently he's always had a reputation for being street-smart."

"Then he should keep this a secret," I said.

Mom laughed. "I'll pass that on."

"You will?"

"On second thought, no. But I take it you didn't see any suspicious characters?"

"Only Sheldon Gunn," I said.

Mom laughed again and said good-bye. I picked up my spoon, but found I was no longer hungry.

7

L ater that day I had the bracelet in my hands and was examining the silver heart, just a tiny shiny thing with no marks or other features, when the doorbell rang. Some dogs get excited when that happens—maybe having to do with ancient guarding genes wrapped in their DNA—but not Pendleton, who dozed on beneath the kitchen table. I pressed the button on the wall speaker and said, "Hello?"

No reply. I remembered that for listening you had to let go of the button, so I did, and heard nothing, probably because whoever was there had already spoken, so I pressed the button and said hello all over again, and then let go.

"Hey—it's me, Ashanti." Ashanti at the door? That was a first. She sounded impatient. "I've got your homework."

"Great, thanks," I said. "I mean, not great, actually,

like, homework, you know? But, ah . . . be right down."
I pushed the button somewhere in the middle of that
bumbling around, so what Ashanti ended up hearing
was anybody's guess.

I went downstairs, unlocked all the locks, and opened
the door. There was Ashanti, looking very cool in a
short black jacket, black jeans, and a baseball cap with
Princeton on the front. And it was raining, the street all
wet like it had been raining for some time: I hadn't even
noticed.

"Hi," I said, "thanks for, uh . . ."

Ashanti stepped into the entryway, out of the rain,
unslung her backpack, and started rummaging inside.

"How was practice?" I said.

Ashanti shrugged, at the same time spilling some papers on the floor. She stooped to pick them up, and just
like in some stupid movie, I was stooping, too, and we
bumped heads.

"Ow," Ashanti cried. As did I, and then we were
both rubbing our heads. She gave me an angry look.

"Sorry," I said, although was it really my fault?

"Sorry doesn't—" she began, and then glanced down,
and there among the scattered papers lay the bracelet,
which I seemed to have carried downstairs and dropped
during all that stooping and head bumping. I stooped
once more, now for the bracelet, and so did Ashanti.

No head bumping this time, but Ashanti and I both touched the silver heart at the same time. Right away a shock went through me, like an electric charge, all the way down to the tips of my toes and back up again.

"Ow!" I said again.

"What was that?" said Ashanti.

"Did you feel it too?"

"Of course I felt it," Ashanti said. "Why wouldn't I feel it?"

"Well, um."

She crouched down, eyed the bracelet, still on the floor. "What is that thing?"

"A friendship bracelet."

"Are batteries in it?"

"No." But I hadn't thought of that, couldn't be sure.

Slowly she reached out with her index finger and touched it. Nothing happened. "Must've been static electricity," Ashanti said, "but to the max." She gave me a close look. "Did that T-shirt just come out of the drier?"

The T-shirt I was wearing—one of my favorites, with a picture of a dancing cartoon frog on the front—had in fact come from a pile on the floor of my bedroom, so I said no. Plus, I really wasn't completely clear in my mind about static electricity, wondered if that could explain what had been going on with me, the headaches, the red-gold beam, all that, and was also wondering how to ask Ashanti for some sort of definition without sounding like a total dork, when I noticed she was looking kind of ashy, the normal glow of her skin suddenly gone.

"Are you all right?" I asked.

"Of course," she said. And then, more quietly, "Wouldn't mind a glass of water."

We got the papers sorted out, I put the bracelet back on, and we went upstairs and into the kitchen.

"That's one big dog," Ashanti said, hanging back a little.

"His name's Pendleton." Under the table, Pendleton opened an eye.

For most of my life until recently, we'd had big five-gallon water bottles delivered every two or three weeks, but now the cooler stood empty in the corner, my parents having decided that bottled water was the wrong way to go from the environment's point of view. I filled a glass from the tap at the sink, where there was now a filter down underneath, and set it in front of Ashanti. She drank half of it in one gulp, the glow returning to her skin almost right away.

"A dog bit me when I was little," she said.

"That won't happen with Pendleton."

His eye closed.

Ashanti glanced around the kitchen. "What do they do?" she said. "Your parents."

"My mom's a lawyer. My dad's a writer."

"What does he write?"

"Like, novels."

"Published?"

"Yeah."

"Cool."

She drank more water, tilting her head back a little. Ashanti was beautiful, no doubt about that, every feature just perfect, as though extra effort had gone into designing her. No grandmother had ever told her she'd grow into a beautiful woman one day: it was too obvious for words.

"And your parents?" I said.

Ashanti looked down her beautiful nose at me. She didn't answer the question, instead saying, "Ms. Kleinberg talked about you at practice today."

"Yeah?" And suddenly I knew what was coming: Ms. Kleinberg was kicking me off the team.

"She said you were a heady player."

Heady? Me? Ashanti had to be putting me on, right? But there was no sign of that on her face.

"Weird."

"What's weird?"

"What you just said. Me being heady."

"I didn't say it. Ms. Kleinberg did."

Meaning what? Ashanti didn't think I was heady,

maybe even thought the opposite? Intimidating and prickly: my very first impression of Ashanti, and nothing had changed. But now I was getting a bit prickly myself.

"Yeah," I said. "I got that."

We gazed at each other, not in a particularly friendly way. A vague idea about my current lack of friends maybe having something to do with my own behavior stirred in my mind and quickly sank from sight.

"How about a snack?" I said.

"Got to split." But Ashanti didn't move, and after a second or two, said, "Like what kind of snack?"

I rose and opened the fridge. "There's leftover Thai," I said.

"From Your Thai?"

"Yeah."

"Not *kaeng phet ped yang,* by any chance?"

"This is your lucky day," I said.

Ashanti smiled. I'd never seen her smile before—and, come to think of it, never seen her look happy. In photos of me I've always got a goofy smile on my face.

I took chopsticks from the drawer, and we ate right out of the carton, taking turns on the dipping-in part.

"It's even better cold," Ashanti said.

"Way better."

"Mr. Nok's a funny guy."

"The owner?"

"He learned English from Mel Gibson movies. He memorized whole chunks. You should hear him do that speech where Mel is firing up the dudes in the kilts before the battle."

I laughed.

"Too bad about what's happening to him."

"Mel Gibson?"

Now Ashanti laughed, too. Her smile was great—made sense of that expression about the kind of smile that lit up a room—but her laugh was harsh and raspy. For some reason I started laughing again, spewing little bits of Thai, which made Ashanti laugh harder. After thirty seconds or so, we calmed down; I sensed that things were different between us now, but couldn't have said in what way.

"Not Mel Gibson," Ashanti said, poking around in the bottom of the carton with her chopsticks. "I'm talking about Mr. Nok. He's closing down."

"Closing the restaurant?"

"Uh-huh."

"Moving it to a bigger place?"

"Nope. He's fed up—talks about going back to Thailand."

"Oh, my God. Fed up about what?"

"Too much naked greed. That's what he told my dad, anyway." Her eyes took on a brief inward look. "My dad's fed up about the same thing."

"I don't get it," I said. Were the customers greedy, maybe not willing to pay enough for such great food?

"A new landlord came in and jacked the rent way up."

"Whoa," I said, struck by an obvious thought.

"Whoa what?"

"This landlord—is his name Sheldon Gunn?"

"Don't know."

"Or maybe the Brooklyn something or other redevelopment project?"

Ashanti shrugged.

All of a sudden, I felt the silver heart warming up against my skin. "Feel this," I said. "The heart."

Ashanti looked at it through narrowed eyes and then reached out. She had long, slender fingers, the nails painted sky blue. "Hey—it's hot."

"Yeah."

"You're sure it's got no battery? Maybe some real tiny one?"

"I'm not actually sure."

Ashanti picked up the bracelet, turned it this way and that, checked both sides of the heart. "It's cooling down."

"Yeah?"

"And there's no sign of a battery." She hefted the heart on her fingertip. "Gotta be platinum," she said. "Heavier than silver and way more expensive—number seventy-eight on the periodic table."

"Wow. How do you know that?"

"We had a test on the periodic table last week."

"Thatcha," I said.

"Comin' atcha," said Ashanti.

Thatcha comin' atcha was a Thatcher thing I'd seen in the halls from time to time but never been part of.

"Platinum, huh?" I said, and reached across the table to touch it. I felt a sudden strangeness in my hand, like a dull throbbing, and froze an inch away.

"Hey!" said Ashanti.

"What?" I said.

"I've got this strange feeling in my hand."

"A dull throbbing?"

"Yeah," Ashanti said. "Kind of like it's building to another shock."

"Me too," I said. Our hands, so close to each other, looked perfectly normal, revealing nothing of what was going on inside. I withdrew my hand. The dull throbbing faded and vanished.

"Gone," said Ashanti. "What's going on?"

"Put the bracelet on the table," I said.

Ashanti set it down. I reached out again, very slowly, and took Ashanti's hand: no throbbing, no shock, nothing. She gazed at the bracelet. "It's got some kind of . . ." She couldn't come up with the word.

Neither could I. But at that moment I was hit by

another of those realizations. "Whatever it is," I said, "you're part of it."

"Can you be more specific?" Ashanti said, back to her intimidating ways. "For once?"

For once? Like we were old friends. "Remember that foul?" I said.

"The one that chinless creep didn't call?"

"Exactly. The thing is . . ." and I launched into the whole story. The homeless woman and her death, the bracelet, the electric ball, the currents to my eyes, the red-gold beam, the $3,100 and what I did with it, the head-aches, the fever, the MRI—everything. I made a complete mess of it, getting events out of order, making no sense. When I finally shut up, Ashanti was gazing at me, eyes wide, mouth slightly open.

"You don't believe me," I said.

Ashanti didn't answer. Instead she picked up the bracelet. Then, slowly, she reached out with her other hand and took my hand in hers. *Kapow!* Right away I got zapped by a shock, and so did Ashanti—I could tell from her face. I tried to snatch my hand away, but she didn't let go; her grip was powerful, much stronger than mine.

"Hey!" I said. "What are you doing?" The shock went on and on, pulsing up and down my body.

"Shut up," said Ashanti. And all at once, the pulsing

subsided, right down to nothing. Ashanti squinted toward the wall. "I don't see it," she said. "Do you?"

"See what?" My hand was all sweaty; so was hers.

"The beam, for God's sake," she said.

"No," I said. "No beam."

"And I didn't feel the electric ball thing."

"Me neither."

Ashanti let go of me. "We only got a partial," she said.

"A partial?"

"Something's missing." Ashanti's eyes shifted, like she was having a thought. "How about we go visit Mr. Nok?" she said.

"There's another carton in the fridge—green curry."

"It's not about that."

"What's it about?"

"I've got an idea."

"I'm listening."

"It's hard to explain."

"Try."

She shook her head. "Let's just do it."

Why not, whatever it was? "Thatcha," I said.

"Comin' atcha."

Fist bump. And since Ashanti still had the bracelet in her other hand, that meant—

"Ow!"

8

I left a note on the fridge: *Gone to Your Thai w/Ashanti (friend from T). Back soon.*

We went down to the street. Night was falling and the rain had stopped, leaving the pavement slick and shiny and streaked with streetlamp reflections, an effect I was more familiar with from movies than from real life. We walked back up the hill and turned onto the street with the halfway house. Maybe it wasn't very nice in there, because guys from the halfway house were always out on the stoop, even in bad weather. This was the halfway house for guys with mental problems. I preferred going by the other halfway house in our neighborhood, the one for inmates on probation, and was glad Ashanti was with me. There were two guys on the stoop, one nodding off, the other reading the Bible—I could tell from the gold edging on the pages. Without even a glance at us, he said, "Roll away the stone, sisters, roll away the stone," as we passed.

We walked in silence for a few yards, and then Ashanti said, "Ever wonder how they get like that?"

"Not really."

"You're smart."

"What do you mean?"

"Because trying to figure it out's a waste of time," Ashanti said. "No one knows."

I glanced at her. Ashanti's face was hard and unhappy. "Is this . . . um, mental illness stuff another thing you take in eighth grade?"

She shook her head.

Dumb question on my part, which I should have known from the get-go: "No one knows" was not a Thatcher-type answer.

Your Thai was on the next block, one of those places slightly below street level, so that all you saw through the window were the below-the-knees parts of the people going by. The kitchen was behind a counter at the back; there were a few tables in front, with only one customer, bent over a steaming bowl. Mr. Nok was chopping a bright-orange pepper and talking on a cell phone at the same time, the phone wedged between his shoulder and ear. He was a very little guy and always wore one of those tall white chef's hats, which should have made him look ridiculous but somehow did not.

"What form? What form?" he was saying. "I fill out all form. All form, many, many time." He sounded agitated and his face looked agitated, his forehead knotted up, but his hands seemed calm, if you could say that about hands, calmly and neatly chopping up the pepper in quick, even strokes. His voice rose. "No attachment! Fax!" He clicked off, swept the peppers into a bowl, turned to us.

He blinked, then smiled, a strange smile, what with his forehead still being so tense.

"Hi, Mr. Nok," said Ashanti.

"Hello, Ashanti." He glanced at me. "And you, young lady always for the *kaeng phet ped yang*." For a second or two, I didn't get what he was talking about; Mr. Nok's pronunciation of the dish was a lot different from mine.

"Yeah, it's awesome," I said. "I'm Robbie. Is it true you're moving or something?"

His smile vanished. Mr. Nok had one of those unlined faces that made it hard to see his true age, but now he looked pretty ancient. "They close me down," he said. "No more *kaeng phet ped yang*." He turned to Ashanti. "No more Mel Gibson."

"Why—" I began, but at that moment a fax machine at the end of the counter whirred into action. Papers began shooting into a tray—and spilling out, since the tray was full, and fluttering to the floor at my feet. I bent down, picked them up, and placed them on the counter, but not so quickly that I missed the letterhead on the top sheet—Jaggers and Tulkinghorn—hey! Mom's firm! Before I could read any more, Mr. Nok reached over and grabbed the sheet of paper. He scanned it, wincing like he'd felt a sudden pain inside. Then he laid it down behind the bowl of peppers and out of my view.

"But, Mr. Nok," Ashanti was saying, "what about somewhere else? There must be other places you could rent."

Mr. Nok shook his head. "Here is perfection," he said, looking around the small space, low-ceilinged, not well lit, smoky-smelling, and even a bit dirty, to tell the truth. "This is my dream, my American dream." His eyes welled up, and two tears rolled down Mr. Nok's smooth face, leaving glistening tracks.

I leaned close to Ashanti and spoke in her ear. "Can you read that letter?" I said. She rose on her tiptoes, trying to see over the bowl of peppers, then shook her head. "It might be important," I said.

At that moment, Ashanti did something I didn't expect at all. Her eyes on Mr. Nok's unhappy face, she grabbed me hard by the wrist—the bracelet wrist. The shock followed at once, and this time it brought the power, although the electric ball came and went in seconds, and so did the blurring of my vision. I got the feeling, rare for me, that I knew exactly what was coming next. All the power, the power in the bracelet, or in me, or both, was about to pass into Ashanti, and this time the red-gold beam would shine from her eyes.

But that was not what happened. Oh, maybe the power-passing-from-me-to-her part was right, because I felt a slight weakness in my knees, but no red-gold beam shone from Ashanti's eyes. Instead she suddenly . . . grew? Was that it? Not wider or bulkier, just taller, by about six inches or so. I glanced down and saw that her feet were off the floor. She was hovering in the air, with no visible means of support. And the expression on her face, that face so seldom smiling—I'll never forget it: astonishment blossoming into joy. Mr. Nok, wiping his damp cheeks on the back of his sleeve and reaching for another bright-orange pepper, didn't seem to notice. Ashanti rose a little higher, without the slightest effort, and peered over the bowl at the letter. The hovering went on for maybe another ten seconds or so, and then she settled slowly back to the floor—down to earth, was what I actually thought at the time—and landed softly.

We looked at each other. "Did you see that?" Ashanti said, so quietly it was more like mouthing the words.

"Wow," I said, also quietly. *Wow* didn't seem like a good enough word for the occasion, but nothing else came to mind.

Mr. Nok's cell phone rang, and he moved down the counter to talk.

"Let's go," said Ashanti.

We headed toward the door. The lone customer was watching us. Was there suspicion in his eyes? I thought so, but some adults always looked at kids that way.

Out on the street, I said, "You . . . you levitated."

"Yeah."

"What did it feel like?"

"Totally sick," Ashanti said. "Is that your mom's firm, Tulkinghorn and Jaggers?"

"Yeah."

"Who's Egil Borg?"

"Never heard of him."

"He's the one who signed the letter. It says that because Mr. Nok hasn't paid the New Brooklyn Redevelopment Project, they're suing him for treble damages."

"What does that mean?"

"Something bad."

We started walking home.

"How come you wanted to see Mr. Nok?" I said. "Did you know what would happen?"

"No way," Ashanti said.

"You said you had an idea."

"More like an urge," Ashanti said. "I just had to. There was this pressure building in my head, building and building, and I thought the red-gold beam would happen, but it didn't."

"So you believed me about that? The beam and all?"

"Yeah."

"No doubts?"

"Nope."

"But why?" I said. "It's actually not so easy to believe. I'm still having trouble myself."

Ashanti flicked my shoulder with the back of her hand. "Hey! What's wrong with you? Trying to get me to doubt you? A little too late, don't you think, now that I've got this hovercraft thing going?"

I laughed. So did Ashanti. She gave my shoulder another one of those backhand flicks.

"Any pressure now?" I asked. "Inside your head, I mean."

"I know what you mean," Ashanti said. "And the answer's no. The moment I rose up it was all gone, *pffft*, just like that."

"Do you think you could do it again?"

Ashanti closed her eyes, took a deep breath. A moment passed. "No," she said. Her eyes opened. They turned yellow in the headlights of a taxi passing by, then went back to normal, an effect I'd probably seen many times at night, but now inspired a new thought, probably crazy: *there's magic in the world.* "What about you?" Ashanti said. "Can you make the beam happen?"

"No."

"Try."

I tried my best, if trying my best meant squeezing my eyes shut, scrunching up my face, and praying for a headache. No electric ball, no currents, no beam, no change of any kind. I shook my head.

"What if we both touch the heart?" Ashanti said.

"We'll get a shock."

"So what?"

We both touched the heart. Surprise: no shock. Also no beam, no levitation.

"Something extra has to be in the mix," Ashanti said. "Some outside thing makes it happen."

"The New Brooklyn Redevelopment Project?" I said. But that couldn't be right: the New Brooklyn Redevelopment Project had nothing to do with the foul on the basketball court. And what about Tut-Tut? How could there be any connection between those skateboarders and Sheldon Gunn? What did all those events or situations or whatever they were have in common? I didn't know.

"Poor Mr. Nok," Ashanti said. "Comes all this way for his dream, cooks the greatest food in town, and then gets kicked onto the street. There's no justice."

"Whoa! Say that again."

"About Mr. Nok and the American dream and—"

"No. The last part."

"There's no justice?"

"Exactly." I was getting excited. "That's the outside thing, what makes the magic happen!"

"Magic?"

"Or whatever this is. Maybe not magic, but something special." And didn't it have to be special, because of all the injustice around? I suddenly felt the weight of the injustice, as if the whole huge city and all its buildings were pressing down.

"Injustice is the outside thing?" Ashanti said.

"Any other explanation?" I said.

"Sure," said Ashanti. "We're both out of our minds."

shanti lived across the street from me and three or four stoops down. Her apartment was on the ground floor, but it looked a lot like ours: we even had the same kind of fridge. One big difference was all these professional-type photos on the living-room walls, the same beautiful young woman in each of them. Ashanti noticed me staring at them and said, "My mom—back in her modeling days."

"Wow," I said. "She was a professional model?"

"Uh-huh."

"Hey! This one's a *Vogue* cover."

"Yeah."

"Wow," I said again. I'd never seen anyone so beautiful. Ashanti—lighter-skinned than her mother—was beautiful, too, but not like this, so perfect, so dramatic. "She's not a model anymore?"

Ashanti shook her head. "They're like athletes," she said. "All washed-up at thirty-five, sooner in her case."

"What does she do now?" I said.

Ashanti glanced down the hall. "At this very moment?" she said. "Probably resting."

"Oh," I said. I got the impression—maybe later than most people would—that Ashanti didn't feel like discussing her mother. Then—maybe sooner than most people—I found myself asking about her father. "What does your dad do?"

Ashanti's eyes narrowed. "Are you always this nosy?"

"Sorry."

"He's a film editor."

"Yeah? Cool."

"It's not. Mostly he does car commercials." She sat on the couch, flipped open a laptop.

"What cars?" I said.

Ashanti glared at me. "Look. Are you in on this or not?"

"In on what?"

"Helping Mr. Nok."

"How are we going to do that?"

"How? Like you helped that soup kitchen place, that's how."

"But that just happened," I said. "I can't make it happen—didn't we just go through all this?"

"So we give up?" Ashanti said. "Just roll over without a fight?"

"No," I said. Rolling over without a fight sounded bad. "But what are we going to do?"

"That's what we've got to figure out, right?" Ashanti said. She patted the cushion beside her. I sat down. "What's the guy's name, again?" she said.

"Sheldon Gunn."

We looked up Sheldon Gunn. He turned out to be a billionaire, and not just a billionaire but the third richest billionaire in the whole world.

"A billion is what, exactly?" I said.

"A thousand million," Ashanti said. "A one and nine zeroes." She glanced at me. "Hard to get your head around a number like that, huh?"

"Yeah."

"Suppose," she said, tapping at the keyboard, "you took that billion dollars and invested it for a measly three percent return, like in the bank." More tapping. "You'd get thirty million dollars per year. About eighty-two thousand a day. That's if you have one billion. Sheldon Gunn has forty-three, so you'd have to multiply that by eighty-two thousand to find out what he'd be making a day." Tap-tap. "Three million five hundred twenty-six thousand."

"A day?"

"Yeah," said Ashanti. "But that's not good enough for Sheldon Gunn."

"What do you mean?"

"If he was just letting his money pile up in the bank, then he wouldn't be doing what he's doing."

"The Brooklyn redevelopment thing?"

"And God knows what else. That's why we have to do some research. But here's our one hard fact—three million five hundred twenty-six thousand a day's not getting it done for him."

We researched Sheldon Gunn. He owned things, lots and lots, including *Boffo*, the second biggest yacht in the world; all kinds of art; many houses, including castles in Ireland and France; the biggest ranch in Wyoming, and another even bigger one in Argentina. But the center of it all seemed to be the Sheldon Gunn Organization, which was about real estate holdings—tower after tower in New York, Chicago, London, Dubai, and other cities. The New Brooklyn Redevelopment Project was one little arm of the Sheldon Gunn Organization, hardly mentioned at all, except by residents who'd pretty much given up on trying to stop it. Sheldon Gunn also had a wife—his fourth, way younger than him—named Genevieve. There were lots of pictures of Genevieve online, making it easy, as Ashanti said, to trace the course of her plastic surgeries. Maybe it was a bit cruel of us—after all, we didn't know the woman, although she was quoted as saying some funny things, like "Shelley's biggest problem is he never thinks about himself" and "We'd be just as happy in a tiny cottage"—but soon Ashanti and I were laughing and laughing, tears rolling down our faces.

"What's so funny?"

We turned, and there was Ashanti's mother at the opening to the dark hallway, dressed in a white nightgown, buttoned to the top. She looked so different from in the photos. It wasn't that she'd put on weight, which was what you might expect for an ex-model; in fact, she maybe had lost some, even though she'd been skinny to begin with. But the dramatic part had grown much, much stronger, so strong that the beauty part had gotten overwhelmed. Her hair was wild; her cheekbones cast shadows; her eyes were blurry.

"Sorry if we woke you," Ashanti said, her voice flat in a way I hadn't heard from her before. "This is Robbie."

"I wasn't sleeping," said Ashanti's mom. "I was only resting."

"Nice to meet you," I said.

Ashanti's mom seemed to focus on me for the first time. "You're the one who's moving to Paris?"

"No," I said. "Not me."

She nodded. "You wouldn't have liked it anyway—it's changed so much," she said. "Is anyone going to tell me what the joke is?"

"There's really no joke, Mom," Ashanti said. "Just stuff on the net."

"Such as, *par example*?" said Ashanti's mom.

"Things this woman said," Ashanti replied.

"What woman?"

"Genevieve Gunn."

"Née Skallinsky?"

"Yeah, I think so."

"She never made me laugh," Ashanti's mom said. "But I haven't seen her in years."

"You know her?" Ashanti said.

"I knew her," said Ashanti's mom. "Back when dinosaurs roamed Seventh Avenue." She looked at me. "Nice to meet you, too, Robbie. That's a nice name."

"Thanks," I said. "And nice to—"

She'd already turned and vanished down the hall.

Ashanti and I looked at each other. Her nostrils were flared; her face wasn't happy. Maybe her apartment looked a lot like mine, but the air felt different, if that made sense: much heavier.

"Seventh Avenue," I said. "Is that the Fashion District?"

Her expression changed; anger had a lot more energy in it than sadness. "You never stop, do you?" she said.

"Huh?"

"With your personality."

"Huh?" I said again. But then this quick turn of events hit me for what it was—I mean, my personality was me—and the next clear thing I knew—this was after some raised voices on both our parts—I was on the street. My street: home territory, but I felt disoriented anyway and close to tears. I made a conscious effort not to let them flow. I had a pretty good life, with or without friends. Didn't I? Okay, so maybe a tear or two, but there wasn't time for any more of that because when I crossed the street and approached my house, Tut-Tut stepped out of the shadows.

"Tut-Tut?" I said.

He wore his hoodie, torn jeans, plus mismatched sneakers, one white, one black, and both too big for him; also his nose was running.

"R-r-r-r-r-r-r-r-," he said. "R-r-r-r-r . . ."

"Robbie?" I said, guessing what he was trying to say.

He nodded, a very vigorous up-and-down that made me have an unpleasant thought: it was kind of a silent stuttering, as though Tut-Tut were all about stuttering. I brushed that thought away. I knew very well that Tut-Tut didn't stutter inside, in fact had a commanding voice that just couldn't get out.

"I–," he said. "I-I-I-I . . ."

"What is it?" I said. "What's wrong?" Something was wrong—I could see it on his face.

Tut-Tut didn't even try to answer. He just reached out and grabbed my arm with both of his. What was going on? Tut-Tut was squeezing so hard it hurt, and

I was just about to pull away when I figured it out: he was trying to make the shock happen, trying to get hold of that electric thing that had the power to make him talk.

But there was no shock. No electrical ball, no power. Tut-Tut let go. "N-n-n-n-n-n-n-," he said.

"I'm sorry," I said. "I can't make it happen." There had to be injustice in the mix, as Ashanti and I had figured out. But wasn't Tut-Tut's stutter an injustice? How could it possibly be just for him to be afflicted like this? So maybe the whole injustice idea was wrong. What was I missing? I stood on the street, the wind picking up, icy rain starting to fall, and tried to think. No thoughts came. Then I noticed that Tut-Tut was shivering.

"Hey," I said. "Want to come inside?"

"W-w-w-w-," he said.

"I live here," I said, gesturing at the building. "Let's get out of the rain. I can make hot chocolate."

Tut-Tut didn't move, just gazed at me from inside his hoodie, the seams all frayed.

"And we could have a snack," I said, even though I wasn't the least bit hungry myself. "Some leftovers from Your Thai, maybe."

Tut-Tut's look was blank. Was it possible he didn't know about Thai food? More than possible, I thought a moment or two later, a moment or two too late, as usual.

And was there something a little rude or insensitive in even raising the idea of Thai food with Tut-Tut, as if I'd asked him what country club he belonged to? Not that I belonged to a country club myself, although I'd been to one—my uncle Joe's, in New Jersey—the day I had my only golfing experience, the only one I'll ever have, guaranteed.

We stood in the rain, getting wet. It was like I had to find the magic words or something. "Besides," I said, "I've got your flip-flops and spray paint."

I caught a flicker of interest from inside Tut-Tut's hoodie. I took out my keys and opened the door. Tut-Tut moved toward the entrance. At that moment, the other door opened and Mitch, the landlord, came out, unfurling an umbrella. He had a frown on his face and his forehead was knitted, as though he was working on some tough problem—his usual look. Mitch glanced at me.

"Robbie."

"Hi, Mitch."

Then he noticed Tut-Tut, realized that Tut-Tut was with me, and gave him a long look. I went inside, motioning Tut-Tut after me. He followed. I closed the door; by that time Mitch had turned and was walking off.

"The landlord," I said on the way up the stairs. "Not that bad of a guy, really."

Tut-Tut grunted, a single unstuttering sound, actually quite pleasant for a grunt.

I like our apartment, but it's nothing fancy, not as apartments go in this neighborhood. Fancy is high ceilings and polished hardwood floors and Persian carpets and tall windows with amazing views, and we have none of that, except for the hardwood floors. And one Persian rug, not very big, and stained forever by Pendleton during his younger days. All in all, nothing fancy, but Tut-Tut stood in the doorway, amazed.

"It's nothing fancy," I said, maybe not the right remark, but what was? At that moment, Pendleton ambled in. He saw Tut-Tut and shrank back. Tut-Tut shrank back, too.

"Guys," I said. "Everything's fine."

After not too long, I got Tut-Tut to sit at the kitchen table; Pendleton settled in underneath. I made hot chocolate—not in Monsieur Señor's class, but not too bad—poured it into two mugs, and set one in front of Tut-Tut. These were mugs I'd never taken much notice of—I think my mom got them in Vermont—but Tut-Tut seemed mesmerized by his. He ran his fingertip over the shiny glaze and traced the outline of the happy-looking cow.

"Drink up while it's hot," I said, sounding like a mom myself.

Tut-Tut took a little sip. The expression in his eyes changed: he liked it. He took another sip, liked it even more. Were these his first tastes of hot chocolate?

"I'll just go up and get your stuff," I said.

I went upstairs, took Tut-Tut's flip-flops and his spray paint from under the bed. The flip-flops were falling apart, and what good were they in winter? What Tut-Tut needed were sneakers that fit. I had extras in my closet, and our feet looked to be about the same size. The logical thing was to kick off my own shoes and try on the flip-flops, just to make sure, which I did.

Then, as I stood in front of my mirror in Tut-Tut's flip-flops—they fit fine, by the way—something illogical started to happen. I had three or four pairs of sneakers, maybe more, in different colors, and it occurred to me that Tut-Tut, being artistic, might have color preferences, so I called downstairs, "Tut-Tut, come up here for a sec."

Only that didn't quite happen. What came out of my mouth was "T-t-t-t-t-tu-tu-tu-tu-tu-" No matter how hard I tried to say "Tut-Tut, come up here for a sec," I couldn't. I could only sound just like Tut-Tut.

'd never been so scared in my life. This . . . power, or whatever it was—obviously I didn't really understand it, but one thing I'd taken for granted was that it had to be a force for good. Now here I was standing in Tut-Tut's flip-flops, and I couldn't talk. My first reaction was to kick off those flip-flops like they were on fire. Totally crazy, because how could two crappy pieces of rubber or whatever flip-flops were made of have anything to do with stealing my ability to speak? I opened my mouth and tried to say the first thing that popped into my mind, which was, "Please don't let this happen." But all that came out was "P-p-p-p-p-p. . . ."

I saw my face in the mirror, a terrified version of me I hardly recognized. It was like my whole life I'd been standing on a nice safe floor and all the time just underneath there'd been a pit of fire or a nest of snakes or some other horrible something.

"P-p-p-p-p-p-," said this cracking-up me in the mirror. And then, just when I was on the point of collapsing in a screaming heap, I thought of the bracelet. I grasped the silver heart between my index finger and thumb. It was hot, almost too hot to hold, but I held on to it anyway. In fact, I couldn't let go; it seemed to be locking my hand in place. And as I held the silver heart—or it held me—I saw something amazing: wisps of smoke rose from Tut-Tut's flip-flops and they began to melt. I can't be sure about the time, but it seemed to pass very quickly, from the start of melting—a strange, heatless melting—to the complete disappearance of the flip-flops, nothing left at all, not even the smoke.

"Oh, my God," I said. Not "o-o-o-o-o," but the complete sentence, no problem. Meanwhile the silver heart was cooling fast; my grip on it unlocked and let go. "Fourscore and seven years ago," I said, just to make sure I was back to my old talking self. Fourscore and seven years ago—however many years that was, exactly—came through loud and clear.

I sniffed the air, smelled a rubbery smell, not too strong. I opened the window, let in the cold wind, and in moments the rubbery smell went away.

Back to normal. But just to be sure, I said, "Our fathers brought forth on this continent a new nation." I took a deep, deep breath and let it out slow. "Everything's going to be all right," I told myself out loud. I went into my closet, chose a pair of white sneakers with navy trim, grabbed the spray paint, and started downstairs. And on the way, I got hit by an idea, maybe obvious, but exciting anyway, all about Tut-Tut and those flip-flops of his, now gone forever. I took the last steps two or three at a time and raced into the kitchen.

Tut-Tut was still sitting at the table, clearly finished with his hot chocolate, because he was holding the mug upside down and examining the bottom.

"Hey, Tut-Tut!" I said.

He looked up. "W-w-w-w-w-," he said. "Wha-wha-wha—?"

Which took the wind out of me; I'd been so sure that the disappearance of those stupid flip-flops would free up his speech. That was the first time I had the conscious realization that the power was a flaky kind of power.

I put the spray paint on the table. Tut-Tut nodded and tucked it away. "And here are these," I said, holding out the sneakers. "They'll fit."

He shook his head.

"Come on," I said. "I don't need them."

"N-n-n-," he said.

"I've got others," I told him. Suddenly it was very important that Tut-Tut took those white sneakers with navy stripes. I couldn't remember where or when I'd gotten them: I'd never even liked the stupid things. Which wasn't the reason I wanted Tut-Tut to have them. Or could it possibly have been a small part of the reason, that I hadn't even been aware of? My dad talked about the subconscious sometimes, this shadow self in each of us that's not always lined up with the conscious self. I remembered hearing that the second three or four hundred pages of *On/Off* were about what the first three or four hundred pages were about, except from the subconscious point of view. But I really didn't understand much about that, and I also didn't want to think that my motive with the sneakers was mixed in any way.

"Look, Tut-Tut," I said, bending down and yanking off those way-too-big cast-offs he was wearing, "just take them. It makes total sense, and I don't want to argue." Tut-Tut's feet were bare, very nicely shaped feet and pretty clean. I slipped on the white sneakers with the navy trim, laced them up, and rose.

Tut-Tut gazed down at his feet. He turned them this way and that, viewing his new sneaks from different angles. Then he looked up at me. The perfect word for describing the expression on his face came to me: dignified. It was a dignified expression. And I realized at that moment that Tut-Tut was dignified in all sorts of ways.

"Th-th-th-," he said.

"You're welcome," I told him.

I offered more hot chocolate or something to eat, but Tut-Tut refused. Soon after that, he left, knotting the laces of the cast-offs together and slinging them over his shoulder. I went up to my room, suddenly very sleepy. Just before I fell asleep, I said, "Conceived in liberty and dedicated to the proposition," just to make sure I could. And I could, like a champ.

We had an intrasquad scrimmage at practice after school the next day, Ms. Kleinberg reffing. She divided us up by uniform numbers, odds against evens, meaning Ashanti, number six, was on one team and I, number thirty-one, was on the other. I'd passed her earlier in the halls, and she hadn't looked at me. And now, during the scrimmage, she wasn't looking at me either, just waltzing by a couple of times for easy layups.

"Position, Robbie," Ms. Kleinberg called. "Get those feet in position."

Ashanti took a pass, dribbled down on me again. I concentrated on my feet, trying to get them square to Ashanti's path, but Ashanti's path changed at the very last split second and she blew by me one more time. Easy layup. And again without seeming to see me, or even be aware of my existence. That was the most infuriating part.

"Arms, Robbie—get those arms up!"

Plus I was getting real tired of Ms. Kleinberg yelling at me from courtside. Why couldn't she yell at someone else? Were they all playing like LeBron James? While I was having those thoughts, the ball bounced my way and I grabbed it and headed down the court. For once I hadn't even the slightest wish to pass, only wanted to spring up and jam the ball through the hoop (an absurd fantasy, of course, since I couldn't get within two feet of the rim jumping my highest). And smash the glass to smithereens, too, while I was at it, as I'd seen on TV once or twice—also part of my fantasy, maybe the best part.

But in the end, I didn't even get close to the basket, never mind actually putting points on the board. I'd barely reached the top of the key when Ashanti swept in from the side and stole the ball, just plucking it clean out of the air in mid-dribble.

Ashanti circled around and started dribbling the other way, easily faking out a player or two. I took off after her, so mad I wasn't thinking at all. Ashanti was a way better athlete than me—I was under no illusions about that—but I'm a pretty fast runner, an ability I've never worked on, just had from when I was little. And of course Ashanti was dribbling the ball, and that slows anyone down.

I got closer and closer, till the squeaking of Ashanti's

sneakers on the hardwood seemed to grow very loud, and finally caught up to her just as she was taking that last little stutter step and gathering the ball—with her right hand at the bottom and her left hand on the side, the way Ms. Kleinberg had taught us—before going up for the shot. I reached in for the ball, trying to knock it away from her just as she'd knocked it away from me, but I missed completely, hitting her in the side instead. Then somehow our legs got tangled up. We both went flying—the gym spun in a complete three sixty in front of my eyes—and crashed down on the floor, real hard.

We lay there side by side, making those noises people make when they're hurt. But not badly hurt; at least I wasn't. The other kids came running up. Ashanti turned to me—our heads were only a couple of feet apart—and glared.

"You're a pain in the ass, you know that?" she said.

"Right back at ya," I said. Pretty lame, I know, but nothing better occurred to me.

Ashanti rose with a grunt of pain. Then, not actually looking at me, she held out her hand. I took it. She helped me up, just the way the jocks do it on TV.

Ms. Kleinberg blew her whistle. "Ashanti shooting two," she said.

We took our places around the key, Ashanti at the line.

Ms. Kleinberg glanced at me. "Nice aggressive play, Robbie," she said. "Sometimes a foul's the right move."

She handed Ashanti the ball. Ashanti hit two. I took the ball, inbounded it to our other guard, and headed down the floor. Ashanti elbowed me as I went by, but not hard, in fact sort of friendly-like, if elbowing could ever be friendly. I suddenly got hot—if that's what it was: my first-ever time being hot, so I couldn't be sure—and hit three quick baskets before the final whistle. No electric ball, no red-gold beam for aiming. Just me, firing it up there.

Ashanti was waiting for me on the street when I left school. She gave me one of those cool gazes of hers, looking down, on account of her height advantage. "There's stuff about you I don't like," she said.

"I picked up on that," I said.

Then came a surprise. Ashanti shook her head and started laughing. "See?" she said. "And then you do something like that."

"Like what?" I said.

"Doesn't matter," she said. "Whether we like each other or not, I mean. The point is we're in this together."

"In what?" I said.

Ashanti didn't answer, waited for some kids coming out of Thatcher's front door to go by. Then she came a little closer, lowered her voice. "Stopping the New Brooklyn Redevelopment Project, for God's sake! What else?"

"Stopping the project? What are you talking about?"

"Do you think it's just Mr. Nok and that soup kitchen? Sheldon Gunn is driving people out of their places all over town."

"How do you know that?"

"Because of this blog I found."

"What blog?"

Just as Ashanti started to answer, Ms. Kleinberg came through the door. She saw us, paused for a moment, then came down the steps, quick and light on her feet. "Way to leave it on the court, girls," she said as she went by. "Nice practice." She crossed the street and went around the corner, moving at twice the speed of all the other pedestrians.

"Leave what on the court?" I said.

"No clue," said Ashanti.

"Maybe that was some sort of guidance," I said.

"Possibly."

"But getting back to the blog."

Ashanti took out her phone, pressed some buttons. "Sheldon Gunn Is a Monster dot-com," she said. We gazed at the screen, waiting for the page to pop up. "Hey!" she said. "What the . . . ?"

I leaned closer, read the message: *The page you are looking for can no longer be found.*

"Are you sure you entered it right?" I said.

She gave me a quick glare. "Yeah, I'm sure." But she tried again. Same message.

"Can you remember what was on it?" I said.

"Not the specifics," Ashanti said. "There was all this stuff about people getting kicked out of their apartments, little businesses that can't make the new rent, that kind of thing, but I don't remember the . . . wait a minute—is there something called the Red Goat?"

"It's a bar."

"Where?"

"Near the canal. My dad and some of his writer pals used to go there, but then advertising guys started showing up. They didn't get along."

"Why not?"

I didn't know. Meanwhile, we'd started walking, but not toward the brownstones down the street where I could see those two nannies sitting on a stoop and push-pulling their strollers. Instead, with no discussion, we were headed the other way, toward the canal.

We have this canal in Brooklyn. Long ago the Dutch fished and went clamming in its clear waters—I learned that at Joe Louis. No fish or clams now, of course: the water's that same sickly green you see in the test tubes of mad scientists in the movies. As Ashanti and I crossed the bridge, a big fat gas bubble burst on the surface, and then another, rising up from the putrid depths. We caught the familiar stink, way worse in summer than now.

"Eww," said Ashanti.

The Red Goat stood across the street from the bridge, one of those lopsided old buildings you see in Brooklyn sometimes, leaning like a drunk, which was kind of appropriate. A big carved red goat hung over the door.

"Cool sign," Ashanti said.

"Yeah, and the building leans like—" I began to say, letting Ashanti on my little joke, but stopped when the door opened and a man came out with a stepladder. He wore heavy work boots, shorts, and a T-shirt—one of those guys who dressed like it was summer all year round. He had a shiny bald head and a full beard, a look you saw from time to time, and which I found vaguely nauseating. In a moment or two, he'd set up the ladder and was at the top, working on the Red Goat sign with a screwdriver. He took out some screws, stuck them in his teeth, grabbed the goat by its front legs, and pulled. The goat came free. The guy put it on his shoulder and climbed down the ladder.

We crossed the street. "Hi," I said. "Cool goat."

The guy grunted and started toward the door.

"Cool goat" maybe hadn't been the way to go, and time was running out, since we couldn't follow him inside.

"Um," I said.

And then Ashanti saved the day. "We're doing a school project," she said. "All about the New Brooklyn Redevelopment Project."

The guy stopped and turned. "Got nothin' to say about those"—and then came a word that kids are not supposed to utter, although adults do all the time.

"How come?" said Ashanti.

"How come? Because they're the"—another one of those words—"that's puttin' me out of"—and one more—

"business. Why do you think I'm taking down Big Nanny?"

"That's the goat's name?" I said.

"Since 1959," said the guy.

"It's a great name," I said.

"Well, forget about it," said the guy. "Over, kaput, finito."

"Because of the New Brooklyn Redevelopment Project?" Ashanti said. It hit me that maybe she outdid me a bit when it came to sticking to the point.

"Better believe it," the guy said, plus some more bad language.

"What happened?" Ashanti said.

"Huh?" said the guy. "What's it to you?"

"Like we said," Ashanti told him. "A school project."

He shifted Big Nanny on his shoulder in an impatient sort of way. A neck chain that had been hidden under his T-shirt popped out, with silver letters hanging on the end: *Duke*. "How's talkin' to a couple of school kids gonna help me?"

"Well," Ashanti said, "there's getting your story out there."

"Yeah," I said. "Like, fighting the PR war."

"PR war?" said Duke. "Are you nuts? Those jerks own the PR companies."

"They do?" I said.

"They own everything. That's the point."

"They don't own you," I said.

"Only 'cause I'm not worth anything no more," Duke said. "This is late-stage capitalism—don't they teach you nothin' in school no more?"

That shut me up. I'd never heard of late-stage capitalism, and what if they really weren't teaching us anything in school? But it didn't shut Ashanti up.

"They don't own us," she said.

Duke squinted at her. "I was like you once," he said. "Just wait." He went inside the Red Goat and slammed the door.

Ashanti and I looked at each other. "Have you gotten to late-stage capitalism?" I said.

"Nope."

"Maybe it comes in high school."

"Can't wait." We moved away from the Red Goat. "We're nowhere," Ashanti said.

"Uh-huh."

"We need info."

"Right. What was the name of that blog?"

"Sheldon Gunn Is a Monster dot-com. Where did the stupid thing go?"

"You mean where do blogs go when they're gone?"

"Yeah."

"No clue," I said. "Do you know any geeks?"

"Practically everyone I know is a geek," said Ashanti. "Present company excluded, of course."

"Hey. I'm just tremendously honored."

"You're more of the sarcastic type."

"And you?" I said.

Ashanti's eyes shifted. For a moment she looked very still and quiet, her aggression or chippiness or whatever you wanted to call it disappearing. "Maybe the same," she said. At that moment, I actually did feel honored, if just the tiniest bit.

"The kind of geek we're looking for," I said, "is the techno-expert-type."

Her face brightened. She snapped her fingers. Ashanti turned out to be one of those people capable of loud finger snaps. "Silas," she said.

"Who's he?"

"This kid I sort of know. Couldn't be geekier."

"He's at Thatcher?"

Ashanti shook her head. "He doesn't go to school."

"Meaning he's already graduated from college?"

"Who said anything about college? Silas is my age. He's a homeschooler."

When it comes to homeschooling, I think of rural places, like farms and ranches, or at least the burbs, but Silas lived in an apartment building just tall enough to be called a high-rise, about a ten-minute walk from the Red Goat. DOORMAN OFF DUTY read a notice, which suited me fine: I can open my own doors, don't need some guy dressed like an extra from *The Nutcracker* to do it for me. In the outer lobby, Ashanti looked up the apartment number and pressed the buzzer.

A few seconds passed and then a voice came through the speaker: "Stand and deliver."

Yes, a geek for sure.

"Silas?" Ashanti said.

Through the speaker: "The one, the only."

"It's Ashanti. Let me in."

Silas's voice rose a few notes. "Ashanti?"

"That's what I said."

"You want to come up?"

"Right again."

"It's just me here."

"Hitting the books?"

"Not exactly."

Ashanti rolled her eyes. "Silas?"

"Yeah?"

"Press. The. Buzzer."

Bzzz. We went into the inner lobby and rode the elevator to the sixth floor. Silas's apartment was at the end of the hall. He was standing by the open door in one of those toes-out postures, a roundish, red-haired kid with freckles, about Ashanti's height. Silas was dressed like a Thatcher boy—khakis and a collared shirt—except for one detail: he also wore a bow tie. He had one of those very expressive faces, like an actor. Right now it was expressing awkward surprise.

"This is Robbie," Ashanti said as we drew closer. "Robbie, Silas. Silas, Robbie."

"Hi," I said.

"Um," said Silas.

By that time we were at the door. Silas rocked back and forth.

"Haven't seen you in a while," Ashanti said.

"Day before Thanksgiving," Silas said. "Schermerhorn subway station. You said you hated turkey."

"Right," said Ashanti. "There's that photographic memory."

"Well," said Silas, "it's not exactly photographic, if by photographic you mean—"

"We don't really have a lot of time," Ashanti said, "since we're on our way home from school and all, so if you'll just invite us in, we can get started."

"Get started on what?" Silas said.

"Sheldon Gunn Is a Monster dot-com is—" Ashanti said.

"I agree," said Silas.

"About what?" Ashanti said.

"Sheldon Gunn."

"You know who he is?" I said.

"He bought the building where my mother works, and raised the rents," Silas said. "Her boss says he'll have to close the business."

"Maybe not," I said.

"What do you mean?" said Silas.

I explained about the missing blog. Soon we were in Silas's bedroom, a small, tidy bedroom in a small apartment that was messy everyplace else. Silas sat in front of his computer, tapping away. I sat on a stool. Ashanti lounged on the bed.

"Who's that on the wall?" Ashanti said.

"Turing," Silas said, not taking his eyes off the screen.

"Who's he?" I said. The Turing guy had heavy dark eyebrows and wore a tweed suit.

Silas turned in surprise. "Turing? You don't know Turing? We wouldn't be doing this without Turing."

"Doing what?" I said.

"Anything on computers."

"He invented computers?" I said.

"I thought that was Bill Gates," said Ashanti.

Silas looked at her, then at me. "Where do you guys go to school, again?"

"Thatcher," we said.

"You have to pay?"

119

We nodded.

He shook his head, then went back to work.

"How's homeschooling?" I asked after a minute or two.

"Not bad," said Silas, one finger up in the air, hesitating, then coming down decisively on a key. "Calculus is pretty cool."

"You're learning calculus?" I said.

"I needed it for this app I'm working on," said Silas.

"What does it do?" I asked.

"Well," he said, his voice suddenly deepening into a manly register, then squeaking back up to where it had been, "there are some bugs to iron out, but it's for opening combination locks."

"How?" I said.

Silas turned to me, rubbing his hands, his face pinkening with excitement. "You load the app onto your phone, then point the phone at the lock."

"That's it?"

"The combination pops up on your screen."

"Wow," I said.

"It's a few weeks away," Silas said, "but I can show you some of the code, if you like."

"Maybe some other time," Ashanti said, getting off the bed. "Right now we need you working on the blog thing."

"That?" said Silas. "It's all done." He hit a key. The printer on his desk came to life. "Name, social security number, address, e-mail, phone, and credit report."

"What are you talking about?" Ashanti said.

"The blogger who runs Sheldon Gunn Is a Monster dot-com," said Silas. "Isn't that what you wanted?" A sheet of paper slid into the tray. Silas took it out and handed it to me.

And that was when we got a shock, the surprise kind of shock and the literal kind. In the exchange, while Silas and I were both still touching the paper, the electric ball hit me, the hardest hit yet, but also the quickest to go. At the same instant, Silas cried out in pain, and a split second later, the sheet of paper burst into flames. We both snatched our hands away; the burning page glided down to the floor, was mostly ashes by the time it landed. Ashanti stamped out the remaining embers.

Silas backed away, his mouth wide open in a big, silent O.

"You all right?" I said. "Headache, but now it's gone?"

He rubbed his head, nodded. "But how did you—" He glanced at the ashes on the floor, just a few, hardly noticeable. "What—what's going on?"

We sat him down, started telling our story. Silas had that easy-to-read face, so it was obvious at first that he didn't believe us. But his expression started to change when I showed him the bracelet and he felt the silver heart, much warmer than it should have been.

"It's shaped like a heart," he said.

"How observant," said Ashanti.

"Not a real heart, of course," Silas said. "Just the common misrepresentation." Ashanti rolled her eyes. Meanwhile Silas had the heart on his fingertip. "Too heavy to be silver," he said.

"Platinum, right?" said Ashanti.

"More likely palladium or rhodium," Silas said. "We could expose it to various altering agents, I suppose, or get some electromagnets and—"

"Silas!" Ashanti said. "You're missing the point."

"What's the point?"

"It has power—that's the point," she said.

Silas's face wrinkled up, a very unpleasant look on him, showing he wasn't buying it. "So if I put it on, I'd have the power?" he said.

"For God's sake," Ashanti said.

But I slipped off the bracelet and handed it to Silas. "Let's see," I said.

He put on the bracelet. "Now we're friends, right?" he said.

Ashanti and I ignored him. We sat in Silas's bedroom, waiting for something to happen.

"Nothing's happening," Silas said. Time passed. "Do you think bored people live longer?" he said. "Or would it be the other—whoa!"

"Whoa?" we said.

"This thing is getting super cold," he said. "Ow! That hurts." And he yanked off the bracelet, threw it on the bed. Ashanti and I both touched the heart. It felt icy, but warmed up very fast, back to room temperature.

Ashanti and I exchanged a glance. She put the bracelet on her wrist. We gazed at the heart, resting against her skin.

"It's happening again," she said quietly, and then, louder, "Ow." She took off the bracelet and gave it to me. The icy heart warmed up. I put it on. The heart lay against my skin, rose to the temperature of my own body, and stayed there.

"Wow," said Silas. "Talk about data points."

"What does that mean?" I said.

"Too soon to say," Silas said. "But something's going on, no doubt about it. Tell me the whole story again."

We told him the whole story again.

"Hmmm," he said.

"Meaning you're in?" said Ashanti.

"In what?"

"With us."

"Us?"

"Me and Robbie."

His eyes went to me, back to Ashanti. Sometimes boys look scared for no reason.

"What are you planning?" he said.

A good question. There was silence for a few moments. Ashanti and Silas both seemed to be looking at me, like I had the answer or something, which was pretty far from the story of my life so far. But then, out of nowhere, I did have it.

"How does robbing from the rich and giving to the poor sound?" I said.

shanti and I took the elevator down to the lobby in Silas's building, a fresh printout in my hand. I'd plucked this one out of the tray myself, Silas refusing to touch it, even though Ashanti said there'd be no shock this time.

"What makes you so sure?" he'd said.

"I just am," she'd told him.

The elevator doors slid open, and we walked out. A woman was waiting to get on: red-haired, roundish, not a doubt in my mind about who she was. She gave us a sharp-eyed glance as we went by.

"Do you think she knows about the app?" I said when we were on the street.

"Nope," said Ashanti. "But that's not our problem."

"What is?"

"Robbing the rich," Ashanti said. "The giving to the poor part sounds easy enough, but how are we going to rob the rich? We know the power won't turn on without injustice in the mix. So what's the solution, exactly?"

I didn't know. "We'll just have to give it a shot," I said.

Ashanti thought for a moment or two. "Sounds like a plan," she said.

It did to me, too. We were dealing, after all, with a flaky power; or it was dealing with us—a scarier interpretation that I banished instantly from my mind.

The blogger's name was Heinz Mott. He lived over a deli on Flatbush Avenue and had a credit score of 620, whatever that meant. It was after five when we got there, so it seemed like a good idea to call home, which we both did. No answer at either place. We both left messages saying we were with each other and on the way home, very close to the whole truth and nothing but.

A small door stood by the deli entrance; lights shone through a window on the floor above. Ashanti was just raising her hand to press the buzzer when the small door opened and a man came out, struggling with some suitcases. There was something rabbity about his face; and like the White Rabbit, he seemed to be in a big hurry, such a big hurry that he bumped into Ashanti and lost his grip on one of the suitcases. The suitcase was battered and cheap-looking, had duct tape reinforcement here and there, but not enough, because it popped open.

He turned surly right away, the surly-rabbit combo turning out to be a pretty unpleasant sight. "Can't you stupid girls watch where you're going?" he said. He crouched down and started tossing stuff back into the suitcase: mismatched socks, frayed T-shirts, lots of papers, some bundled together and some loose, an envelope. The envelope got away from him, came drifting on a breeze over to me. He didn't seem to notice.

As I picked it up, I couldn't help seeing the name of the addressee: Heinz Mott. And, whoa! What was this? The sender's name, up in the top left-hand corner: Jaggers and Tulkinghorn. I kind of slid the envelope behind my back, but without the slightest intention, at least at that moment, of not giving it back.

"You're Heinz Mott?" I said.

He turned quickly to me, the way people do when suddenly scared. "How do you know my name?"

"A long story," I said, "but it's good to meet you. We've got some questions about your blog."

He went still, a ratty bedroom slipper sliding through his fingers and into the suitcase. "Blog?"

"Yeah," Ashanti said. "Sheldon Gunn Is a Monster dot-com."

He rose, glancing quickly around. "Shh. Keep your voice down."

"Huh?" said Ashanti.

There was no one around except for maybe a few

dozen people or so, all of them the normal kind of people you'd see on Flatbush Avenue, meaning just about anyone from anywhere on the whole planet; and that wasn't counting all the motorized traffic, of course. But no one seemed the least interested in our conversation: that was the point. An old lady unwrapping a candy bar came out of the deli. She moved carefully around a pair of tighty whiteys lying by the suitcase and kept going.

"The thing is," Ashanti said, "how come the blog's not up anymore?"

"I don't know about any blog," he said.

"But you are Heinz Mott?" I said.

He gazed down at me, although not far down, since he wasn't very tall. "Who are you people? What do you want?"

"We're working on a school project," I said. "All about the New Brooklyn Redevelopment thing."

"And we were checking out your blog and then it disappeared," Ashanti said. "We need the list of all the people getting forced out."

Heinz Mott's mouth started doing this strange twitchy thing. "List?" he said. "Where would I ever get a list like that?"

"Good question," I said.

"Yeah," said Ashanti. "Let's start there—where did you get the list?"

His mouth twitched a little more. Then he turned and started flinging stuff in the suitcase, wildly now.

"Also," I said, "why do you call Sheldon Gunn a monster?"

"Do you know him personally?" said Ashanti.

"Know him personally? There is no personally with the likes of him." Heinz Mott rose, fumbling with his suitcases. A taxi appeared in the traffic stream. New Yorkers often sound desperate when they're hailing a cab, but I'd never heard one as desperate as Heinz Mott.

"Taxi!" he screamed. "Taxi!"

The cab pulled over. Heinz Mott yanked the back door open, jammed in the suitcases, crawled in.

"Wait a minute," I said. "We need to—"

"You can't just—" Ashanti began.

Heinz Mott slammed the door closed. The cab drove off. Another car honked. The cab honked back.

"We could jump in another cab and follow him," Ashanti said.

I got the feeling that that only worked in the movies. Plus I had two dollars in my wallet. "How much money have you got on you?" I said.

Ashanti dug in her pocket. "Fifty-five cents."

"Then that's that."

We watched the cab getting away, but we weren't the only watchers. A few parking spaces down from us I saw a fair-haired, square-jawed man on a motorcycle doing the same thing. Then he put on a helmet, kicked the starter pedal, and swerved into the stream of traffic. The light on the next corner turned red, the taxi already across. The motorcycle shot through. More honking.

"So what do we do now?" Ashanti said.

"No idea," I said with a shrug, and somewhere in that shrug became aware of the envelope, still in my hand.

I stepped into the light shining through the deli window, examined the envelope. It had already been slit open at the top, so this wasn't quite the same as opening someone else's mail, at least in my mind at that particular second. Was the letter inside? Yes.

I unfolded it. "Dear Mr. Mott," it began. Then came a confusing paragraph where the phrase "cease and desist" was repeated a couple of times, and after that a signature: Egil Borg. And his title: Associate, Litigation.

"Same guy who wrote to Mr. Nok?" Ashanti said.

"Yeah." I read the letter a few times, felt Ashanti reading along with me over my shoulder.

"What's he trying to say?" Ashanti asked.

"Don't know," I said. "It could be about suing unless the blog goes away."

"Where do you see that?"

I pointed to a sentence. "Maybe here."

Ashanti shook her head. "Remind me not to go to law school."

"Deal." I started to fight my way through the letter

one more time. And then, above that impossible paragraph, I noticed a simple thing. The date: July 8 of last summer.

"Hey!" I said.

"Meaning Heinz Mott didn't cave," Ashanti said.

"Not until yesterday," I said. "Wonder what happened in between."

"Have to ask Egil Borg," Ashanti said.

We both laughed, but not our usual full-bodied-tending-toward-giddy laughter, more a quiet sound that petered out quickly.

Getting late, getting cold: we decided to take the subway. But when we reached the nearest station, it was closed for track rehabilitation, so we kept walking, and on a fairly sketchy block that was new to me, a big guy stepped out of the shadows between two buildings and said, "Interested in a little smoke, ladies?"

We picked up the pace, saying nothing. But he followed us; I could feel his gaze right between my shoulder blades.

"Smoke?" he said again. He had that low, intimate, street drug dealer way of talking, where the sound still somehow carries plenty well enough. Street drug dealers were an occasional fact of life, and Ashanti and I kept doing what we were supposed to do, which was to keep walking and ignore him completely.

He kept following us. We picked up the pace some more. His soft, padding footsteps were soon joined by others. I couldn't stop myself from glancing back, and I didn't like what I saw: another guy had joined him, not as big, but with a look that scared me, a look that included a teardrop tattoo on his cheek, which was supposed to mean you'd killed someone.

"These girls don't seem so interested in smoke," the first guy said.

And then came the voice of the second—the teardrop guy—a scary, stoned kind of voice. "Maybe they just wanna make a donation," he said.

The big guy laughed. "Yeah—you girls look like you can afford a nice donation."

"Generous," said the teardrop guy.

The big guy laughed some more. "You girls generous?"

I sensed quicker movements behind me, and right after that I felt heavy breath on the back of my neck. It was too much.

"Run!" I yelled to Ashanti, and took off.

Ashanti took off, too. We were fast runners, me and Ashanti, but those two guys blew by us almost right away, and whirled around to face us. We skidded to a halt.

They were both smiling. "Rude, not answering a

nice, polite question," the big guy said. "Your mommas didn't tell you?"

"You girls generous?" said Teardrop. "That's our nice, polite question."

I could feel Ashanti trembling, or maybe that was me. "We don't want any drugs," she said. "And we don't have any money."

They shook their heads. "Girls with no money have a kind of look," said the big guy. "Not your kind of look."

"Too true," said Teardrop. "You got the rich-kid look."

"We're not rich," I said, trying to keep my voice steady, but without much success.

"Cool," said the big guy.

"Too cool for school," said Teardrop. "So let's just take a real quick peek into those backpacks of yours."

"You can take them," I said right away.

"Just let us go," said Ashanti.

"Let you go?" said the big guy. "We don't even have you yet."

But the next second they both reached out, the big guy grabbing my arm—and digging in his fingers till it hurt—and Teardrop grabbing Ashanti.

"And now we do," Teardrop said.

We struggled to get free, but they were so much

stronger. In a flash, they'd wrestled us into this alley I hadn't even noticed, an alley squeezed between two dark-windowed buildings. I remembered that right about now was when you were supposed to scream your head off, and I tried, but no sound came out. The big guy gave me a push, real hard, and I fell to the ground. Ashanti saw that happen—a furious look crossing her face—and even though Teardrop had both arms around her, she still managed to kick out sideways at the big guy, hitting him on the kneecap.

"Ow," he yelled, and turned toward her, his hand balling into a fist. The expression, to be paralyzed with fear: I understood it now, because that was me, on the ground in this alley. And then I felt the silver heart heating up against my skin. Next would come the electric ball, the power, and somehow we'd be saved. But I didn't feel power, not the slightest bit! The big guy raised his fist. Oh, no. Somehow the horror of what was about to happen unparalyzed me and I found myself scrambling up and diving at the back of the big guy's legs. He lost his balance and fell, knocking Ashanti and Teardrop down, too. And that was the moment—with everyone but me on the ground—when the power did hit at last. Almost immediately the red-gold beam shone from my eyes—I whipped off my glasses as my vision sharpened— and right at the back pocket of the big guy's jeans. Then came a sizzling sound, a burst of flame, and a rolled-up wad of money came popping out, practically landing in my hands. I snatched it up, and meanwhile Ashanti was back on her feet, too.

"Run," she yelled, and we wheeled around toward the entrance to the alley.

But Teardrop bounced up, so quick, and blocked our way. He reached into his jacket. We didn't wait to find out what he was reaching for, just sprinted in the other direction, deeper into the alley. The shadows grew, and the alley got darker and darker, but not before I saw there was no way out: the alley ended in high chain-link fence topped with razor wire. I glanced back and saw two moving shadows in that narrow unlit trap: Teardrop coming fast, something shiny in his hand, and the big guy just behind, limping a little.

"No way out, schoolgirls," the big guy called.

The chain-link fence, barely visible, just a gleam here and there, was only steps away. Maybe we could try to climb it, but what about the razor wire?

Help! Help! Those screams didn't get out, stayed inside my head.

Then Ashanti said, "Robbie! Take my hand!"

What good would that do? But I reached out, took her hand. Almost too late, because Ashanti was already rising off the ground! She squeezed my hand tight. I squeezed hers even tighter. She kept rising, pulling me up with her into the air, over the chain-link fence, and higher.

From below, voices. "What the . . . ?" said Teardrop.

"Must be a hole in the fence," the big guy told him.

After that came lots of swearing, but by then Ashanti and I were almost out of hearing range.

e weren't flying, Ashanti and I, not in the way a bird flies, since there was no flapping of wings, or like a plane, because there was no engine roar, no sense of that tremendous thrust. In fact, what we were doing was very quiet, just a faint whisper of wind in my ears. It came to me: this was soaring, just like in my soaring dream, where I'd soared over Manhattan. This was Brooklyn: that was one difference. Another was that we weren't way up high, over all the rooftops, but were more at the three- or four-story level, drifting along at a slow pace. Through a window I saw a woman having trouble opening a bottle of ketchup. A few windows down, a man in a wife-beater was admiring his biceps in a mirror.

But I noticed those things only in passing. I was totally caught up in this feeling of soaring, the best feeling I'd experienced in my whole life. We were in midair, with nothing supporting us, wafting now over a bunch of forklift trucks parked behind a warehouse, where a foreshortened man sat smoking on a stool. If he looked up, he'd get a big surprise, but of course he didn't. Why would he? Why would anyone?

"Wow," I said. Totally inadequate, but I couldn't think of anything better. I glanced over at Ashanti. There were tears in her eyes. We still held hands, but our arms weren't spread as though we were gliding, because we weren't gliding on a breeze or making any other kind of effort. We were just up there, period. I was excited, thrilled, full of joy, but strangely calm at the same time, my heart beating only a little faster than normal, and even that might have been a leftover from running in that alley and being so scared. Maybe that was the most amazing part of how I felt now: I wasn't scared the least bit. The truth was I felt more confident than all the times I'd felt confident in my whole life rolled into one and multiplied by zillions.

"Let's go higher," I said.

"How?" said Ashanti.

"I don't know," I said, withdrawing my hand from hers in order to make one of those palms-up I-don't-know gestures. Big mistake. The moment I let go, the soaring stopped, like someone had hit the brakes, and then came the sensation of the floor being whisked out from under me—completely crazy, since there was no floor—and I started to fall.

"No!" I screamed.

And had barely got the word out before Ashanti reached down and grabbed me by the collar of my jacket. A slight lurch, like being in a souped-up dragster surging forward, although I'd never been in a souped-up dragster and had no wish to, and then I was back to soaring. Ashanti took my hand with one of hers, let go of my collar with the other.

"You all right?" she said, glancing over at me.

"Yeah."

"Just remember—ray-gun beam operator, that's you. Wingless flyer, that's me."

"It's more like soaring," I said.

"You're correcting me? In this situation?"

"Sort of."

Ashanti laughed. "You never quit, do you?"

Hey! Was that true about me?

We soared, but low, over Brooklyn. Our power was a powerful power, no doubt about that, and yet flaky at the same time. For example, it was already pretty clear that we weren't going to be able to leap tall buildings at a single bound; the best we could manage was cruising around their lower floors. And cruising slowly, by the way.

"Can you make it go faster?" I said.

"How exactly?"

"I don't know." This time I skipped the hand-gesture part.

"Maybe I'll try thinking it," Ashanti said.

"Thinking 'go faster'?"

"Yeah." She closed her eyes tight. We didn't go any faster.

That raised an issue in my mind. "Suppose," I said, "that eventually we want to go down."

"Like, to earth?"

"Just askin'."

Ashanti tried the eyes-closed method again. We didn't descend, stayed at the same altitude, three or four stories up.

"How about changing direction?" I said.

"Nope," said Ashanti, after a few moments. We continued on our plodding course for a while and then started making a gentle right-hand turn around a building that had one of those seedy bars with blackened windows on the first floor and an old man at a computer in the higher-up window we happened to be passing. He looked up from the screen. An amazed expression crossed his face; he rubbed his eyes and looked again just as we passed out of sight. I glanced back, caught a glimpse of him shaking his head—as though to rattle the parts into place—and getting back to work.

"Did you make that turn happen?" I said.

"It must have just happened," Ashanti said. "I was thinking left."

Meanwhile we were drifting by one of those rooftop water towers. Stairs led from the roof to the tower, and on the top step was perched an owl, huge and snowy white. I'd never seen an owl before in real life, but there was no doubt about it. The owl watched us. Weren't owls supposed to have yellow eyes? This owl's eyes were a very pale and faded shade of blue, kind of . . . kind of like the eyes of the homeless woman, except for the bloodshot part. It spread its enormous wings—I'd had no idea that owls were so big—and slowly flapped away.

"I thought for a second it was going to say something," I said.

"This is crazy enough already," Ashanti said. "Better start thinking of some way to get us down. I've got dance at seven thirty, and I can't miss it."

"I didn't know you took dance."

"Let's discuss it later," Ashanti said. "Think."

"What if you breathe out, completely empty your lungs?"

"What good will that do?"

"You know," I said. "Like balloons."

Ashanti pursed her lips and breathed out. Nothing happened; we kept drifting along at the same altitude, passing a sign with one of those blinking arrows pointing down to the store entrance below.

"Balloons, huh?" said Ashanti.

She really could be very aggravating, but was this a good moment for sending back a little aggro of my own? Probably not. I kept my mouth shut.

"Why does this . . . thing have to be so wacky?" Ashanti said, and as soon as she said it we started to drop like a stone.

We both screamed in total fright. Down, down, down we plummeted—the canal seemed to be below us now, and it was rising at warp speed, but the moment before splashdown, we suddenly leveled out and drifted over the water at a leisurely pace.

"I think I'm going to puke," Ashanti said.

I looked down at the target area, slimy yellow-green water kind of reminiscent of puke itself. "Try burping," I said.

"Why?"

"Sometimes it heads puking off at the pass."

Ashanti tried burping. "Hey! It worked." She turned to me. "Thanks."

"Any time."

We skimmed over the canal, staying dry by inches, and, barely moving now, came to a stop on the street running parallel to the water. Not on the street, exactly: we hovered about six inches above the pavement.

And stayed there. The street—same street we'd been on before, I noticed, with the Red Goat on the corner—was deserted, a good thing, since we seemed to be stuck in midair. We stood straight up, kind of flailing at the ground with our feet, to no effect. Ashanti even tried grabbing me by the shoulders and pushing down, but all that did was make her rise.

"What's the opposite of jumping?" I said.

"Huh?" said Ashanti.

"If we could figure out the opposite of jumping, we could get down."

"We can't figure out the opposite of jumping," Ashanti said, "for the simple reason there's no such—"

And then like a balky old elevator, we were in motion again, settling gently down on planet Earth. The street felt strangely hard against my feet, and my body felt strangely heavy. We stood there. The city seemed silent, which was impossible. After a while, normal sounds started up.

"Did that really happen?" Ashanti said.

Could it all have been some sort of hallucination for two? I reached into my pocket, pulled out the wad of drug-dealer cash.

"It really happened," I said.

Down at the end of the block, a battered old van pulled up in front of the Red Goat. Duke, the guy with the shiny bald head and full beard, still dressed like it was summer, got out and went into the bar. A few moments later he returned with Big Nanny on his shoulder. He slid open the side door of the van and lifted Big Nanny inside, then reentered the Red Goat.

One thing about Ashanti and me, there were these moments when we thought as one. Like now: without a word, we were on the move, running down the street, full speed. We skidded to a stop beside the open van. There was Big Nanny, facing out, her mouth slightly open. From up close, she looked kind of mean. I shoved the cash into Big Nanny's mouth, and we took off.

Ashanti and I found a subway station a few blocks away. We hurried down the steps, swiped our cards, and in a minute or two were seated side by side in a half-full car, two schoolgirls backpacking tons of homework after a long day. No one gave us a second look. They didn't have a clue.

14

We got off the train at the stop three blocks from our street and walked home, fast at first, and then, when Ashanti realized that dance was no longer even a remote possibility, slower. We stopped outside her place.

"What are we going to do about telling people?" I said.

"Like who?" said Ashanti.

"Parents, for example."

She shook her head. "Who's gonna believe us? 'Hey, everybody, Robbie and I were soaring around town last night, but forget any demonstration, because we can't make it happen. You just have to believe us.'"

I thought it over. "Got ya," I said.

I let myself into the apartment, slipped off my backpack. "Hi," I called. "Anybody home?" I kind of knew someone was home; you can sense that. But no one answered. I went into the kitchen.

And there were Mom and Dad, seated at the table, both busy with their laptops. They looked up, their heads moving as one when I came in. I got that uh-oh feeling.

"Sorry if I'm a little late," I said.

"If?" said my mom. She looked tired, with purplish patches under her eyes.

"I said I was sorry."

My mom turned to my dad. I started to feel I'd walked into a play that they'd rehearsed for and I hadn't. Did the next stage direction say I should open the fridge and start rooting around? Probably not, but I was hungry—famished, in fact, absolutely starving. I wondered whether this power of ours—mine and Ashanti's although Tut-Tut certainly shared it, too, in some way, and also maybe Silas as well—demanded extra calories. It was a question I would have liked to ask my parents; impossible of course, as Ashanti had pointed out.

"Robbie?" my dad said. "Can you leave that for later? We want to talk to you."

"All right," I said, maybe not clearly, since I was talking around a mini burrito from Paquita's—our go-to Mexican takeout place—left over from who knows when. I sat down at the table.

"So," my dad said, "it, uh, seems to have taken you a while to get home from school today."

"I left a message."

"Right," my dad said. "Good, as far as it goes."

"What Chas is trying to say," said my mom, "is that the message was vague."

"On my way home with Ashanti is vague?" I said. Uh-oh. Maybe that sounded a little too confrontational. Was confrontational the way to go right now? Probably not.

"I'm not sure I understand your tone," Mom said.

I waited for her to go on. She didn't seem to be going on. Did that mean she was waiting for me? My mom, although not a brilliant writer like my dad, was very smart, a fact that sometimes slipped my mind.

"Tone?" I said, and right away knew that was the wrong word, kind of ironic, tone being the issue and the word *tone* digging me in deeper.

"Is something funny?" Mom said.

"No." But I knew my face had betrayed me.

"Let us in on the joke," said my dad.

"No joke," I said, although an insane pressure to laugh and laugh was building inside me and I had no idea why. "Sorry," I said again.

I wasn't one of those kids who got in trouble a lot with their parents; in fact, hardly ever, which added to my confusion. And confusion was at the center of everything, because any account of my after-school activities would lead to what Ashanti and I had agreed were secrets. And for good reason, I could see now: *What were we doing? Oh, not much, just flying around town, that kind of thing.* Now it would sound insolent and disrespectful on top of being flat-out unbelievable.

My mom put her hands in a little steeple, tapped her fingertips together. I'd seen her do that before, pausing over a big stack of papers she was reviewing, and knew it meant she was thinking hard. But now I had the impression that a specific kind of thinking was involved, planning maybe, as though she was tapping into place some structure, like a lobster trap, for example.

"Are you saying we don't have a right to be concerned with your safety?" she said.

"No," I said, and meanwhile that urge to laugh kept growing stronger.

"Good," said Mom. "Because you're twelve years old."

"Albeit a savvy city girl," said Dad.

Mom gave him a look, and before she'd finished giving it to him, his cell phone rang. He squinted at the screen. "Got to take this," he said, and left the room. She watched him all the way, her face unreadable, and then turned back to me. Hey! Was I causing some sort of problem between them?

"Savvy for twelve doesn't mean savvy period, correct?" Mom said.

"Correct."

"So where were you?"

"With Ashanti, just hanging out."

"Hanging out where?"

"Around the school. In the neighborhood."

"Doing what?"

"Nothing special. Hanging out."

Mom had been gazing at me over that little steeple. Now she lowered her hands, rested them on the table. "If something was wrong, you'd tell me?" she said.

Maybe on paper that would have looked like a question, but it sounded more like an order. For some reason, that was enough to set off the laughter. It came bursting out, completely unstoppable. But big surprise: not in the form of laughter. In fact, it came in the form of sobbing. That shocked me and shocked Mom, too: I could see it on her face.

"Robbie?" She rose, hurried around the table. "What is it? What's wrong?"

"Nothing, Mom. Nothing's wrong."

She took me in her arms. Sobbing turned to normal crying, and then quickly petered out, my mom hugging me. It had been some time between parental hugs; was the lengthening of those nonhugging interludes part of growing up?

I pulled away, wiping my face on the back of my

sleeve. My mom didn't quite let go, still had her hands on my shoulders.

"Obviously something is wrong," she said. "What happened tonight?"

"Nothing."

"At school?" she said. "Did something bad happen at school?"

"No."

"Oh, God. Don't tell me you had another one of those headaches?"

"No, Mom. I feel fine." And I did, physically. Emotionally, I felt horribly weak and stupid on account of my little sobbing jag. Would Ashanti ever have melted down like that? No way.

"Did you get into conflict on the way home? Did someone . . . bother you? Harass you? Interfere in any—"

"No, no, no." I stepped further back, out of her grasp.

"Then what were you crying about?"

"I don't know, Mom."

She folded her arms. "You were with Ashanti?"

"Yes."

"The whole time?"

"Yes."

"I'm calling her parents."

"No!"

"No? Why not?"

"Because you'll embarrass me."

"Tough," Mom said, opening a drawer and taking out the Thatcher book. The next moment, she was punching numbers on the phone. I ran up to my room, slammed the door, threw myself on the bed. I thought of texting Ashanti to give her a heads-up, get our stories straight, but didn't bother. I'd had enough conspiring for one day.

I heard my mom's footsteps a few minutes later. She knocked on my door.

"Yeah?" I said.

She came in. "I spoke to Ashanti."

"Oh, my God."

"Because her mother couldn't come to the phone, Robbie, so don't jump to conclusions. But the point is Ashanti confirmed your story, said you just lost track of the time. She takes responsibility, by the way, specifically asked me not to blame you. Also, her mother grounded her, something about missing dance."

Her mother grounded her? That surprised me. Ashanti's mom hadn't seemed like the grounding type. Also, how weird—the whole concept of someone who could actually get airborne being grounded.

My mom took a deep breath, smiled a smile that

seemed forced but was still a smile, meaning the worst was over.

"So," she said, "all I need from you is some assurance this won't happen again. Home by six, unless you've got prior permission. Agreed?"

"Agreed," I said.

Dad appeared, looking pretty excited. "That was van Slyke—his agent wants to meet me," he said. His gaze went to Mom, to me, back to Mom. "Everything sorted out here?"

Mom nodded.

"Excellent," Dad said, rubbing his hands together. His gaze returned to me. "What's that on your wrist?"

"Uh, this?" I said, my arm rising against my own interests to better expose the bracelet.

"It's called a friendship bracelet, Chas," said my mom.

"Yeah?" said Dad. "Who's the friend?"

"Well," I said. "Um."

Mom leaned in for a closer look. "Is that a heart? How adorable."

"Whoa," said Dad. "Meaning the friend is a boy?"

I felt myself suddenly blushing—no idea why, since boyfriends were not in the picture, but it turned out to be the right move.

"Chas?" Mom said, and she laid her finger across her lips to shut him up.

• • •

"The robber barons," said Mr. Stinecki in history class the next day, "is the name given to a group of industrialists and financiers in the latter half of the nineteenth century. Can we name some of them?"

"Rockefeller."

"Carnegie."

"Morgan."

"Vanderbilt."

"Duke."

"Gould."

"Flagler."

"Flagler?" said Signe Stone. "I think I'm related to him."

"Does the development office know?" said Mr. Stinecki.

Maybe that was a joke; if so, no one laughed. Mr. Stinecki was in his second year at Thatcher. There were rumors that he wasn't being asked back for a third.

We spent the rest of the period on the robber barons. We learned that Morgan swatted photographers with his gold-tipped cane, that Gould tried to kidnap a Scottish lord named Gordon-Gordon, almost starting a war between the U.S. and Canada, and that Rockefeller once said, "God gave me the money."

"Any questions?" said Mr. Stinecki.

There were none.

"For homework, in that case—" he began.

And then my hand went up, first time in Mr. Stinecki's class, first time at Thatcher.

"Ah," said Mr. Stinecki. "Robbie?"

"Um," I said. "Are there, like, any robber barons around today?"

"Interesting question. Opinions, people?"

Nobody had opinions.

"Got anybody in mind, Robbie?" Mr. Stinecki asked. "Russian oligarchs, perhaps?"

Russian oligarchs? That zipped right by me. I plunged on. "How about Sheldon Gunn?"

Mr. Stinecki's eyebrows rose. "And what can you tell us about the good Mr. Gunn, Robbie?"

The good Mr. Gunn? Did Mr. Stinecki mean that, or was he just being sarcastic? I didn't know, felt a bit flustered. "Driving people out of their rentals can't be good," I said.

"Can you elaborate?"

Elaborate meant more info, right? "Like Bread."

"The soup kitchen?"

"He raised their rent, so they had to leave."

"You're talking about the New Brooklyn Redevelopment Project?"

"Yeah."

"The somewhat Orwellianly named New Brooklyn Redevelopment Project, might we say?"

What was that? Missed it completely. I heard kids moving in the hall, sensed restlessness at the desks around me. The period was over. I shrugged.

"Not so very far, on second thought," Mr. Stinecki said, "from 'God gave me the money.' So, yes, Robbie, I believe that robber barons still walk among us." He checked his watch. "*À demain,* everybody." *À demain* was how Mr. Stinecki said good-bye. He'd led last year's tenth-grade trip to Provence, supposedly where things started getting shaky for him.

After a slight hesitation—hadn't he been about to give the homework assignment?—we all began filing out. He'd forgotten the homework! There was homework in every subject every day at Thatcher. He was a goner for sure.

"Do you volunteer at Bread?" Mr. Stinecki said as I went by.

"Yeah."

"Excellent. I heard, by the way, that they're staying open, at least for now. Some anonymous benefactor stepped up."

"Yeah?" I said. Was Mr. Stinecki looking at me extra closely? Or was I just paranoid? "That's nice," I said.

• • •

Ashanti and the other eighth-graders had to stay after school for a meeting about their science projects. Eighth-grade science projects were a big deal at Thatcher. A few years before, one kid, now at MIT, had built something that was now in satellite orbit around the earth. Pretty cool, but cooler than Silas's lock-picking project? Not to me.

I walked home by myself, taking the long route by Joe Louis, my mind on Silas's project. Tut-Tut was alone in the school yard again, but not drawing, just squatting there and watching the street. He got right up the moment I appeared and came through the gate. Was he waiting for me? I noticed he wore my old white sneakers with the navy trim.

He stopped a few feet from me and waved, a little circular wave accompanied by a smile. Tut-Tut had beautiful teeth—white, even, not too big or small.

"Hi," I said. "Nice sneaks."

He stopped waving, stuck his hands in the hand-warmer pocket of his hoodie. "Th-," he said. "Th-th-th—"

"Didn't mean for you to thank me," I said. "Just noticing, that's all."

"It-it-it—"

"It's okay?"

"Y-y-y—" He nodded yes.

We stood there for a moment. I could tell Tut-Tut felt uncomfortable, but I didn't feel at all uncomfortable with him. Was that the reason his stuttering no longer had any effect on me? Meaning, his stuttering no longer roused the power, but also that it had no effect on the powerless me, either. I liked Tut-Tut.

"Where do you live?" I said. "Maybe we could walk together."

He pointed down the street, same direction I was heading.

"Let's go," I said.

Halfway to my place, Tut-Tut and I came to the corner where the Quality Coffin Company stood: "Reliable and Dependable Since 1889." Sometimes the delivery doors were open and you could see the coffins inside, but not today. A cold wind was rattling the Quality Coffin sign, and dark clouds were moving fast across the sky. For a moment, I smelled the sea.

Tut-Tut stopped. Home for me lay straight ahead, but he was pointing down the cross street.

"You live down there?"

"Y-y-y—" He nodded. "C-c-c-c-c—" He made a beckoning gesture.

"Okay," I said, and went with him.

We passed some auto repair shops and a vacant lot, and came to a public housing project, three identical dark brick high rises with a strip of lawn in front, the grass brown and sparse. Tut-Tut pointed to a window on the third floor of the nearest building; all the windows were small, and there were no balconies.

"Your apartment?"

"Y-y-y-y-," he said. "W-w-wa-wa-wa-wa—?"

Did he want me to come up? I'd never actually been inside one of the projects, felt nervous about it.

"I-," Tut-Tut said. "I-I-I—" He stopped trying to talk, shook his head. A smile crossed his face, as though in amusement that he kept bumping up against the same problem. Then he made a box shape with his hands and sort of shoved it in my direction.

"You have something for me?"

He nodded.

We walked past an overflowing trash barrel to the door of Tut-Tut's high rise. I heard muffled yelling from somewhere above. Tut-Tut unlocked the door with a key and held it open for me. I got hit by a wave of stuffy and way-too-warm air, air that carried smells of fried food, tobacco smoke, and pee. Tut-Tut made a little after-you gesture. We went inside.

Tut-Tut's building had a small lobby with rows of mailboxes along one wall, some with doors hanging open, some with no doors at all. An old man drinking something from a paper bag watched us cross the lobby to the elevator.

"Pays your money, and you takes your chance," he said.

Tut-Tut frowned and pressed the button. The doors stayed closed. Above them was a panel of lights that were supposed to show the present location of the elevator, none of them lit. Tut-Tut pressed the button again. A creaking sound came from somewhere above, but nothing happened. The man took a drink and wiped his mouth on the back of his sleeve. Tut-Tut waved to me and turned toward the stairway.

The door stood halfway open, held in place by a rag stuffed underneath. The smell of pee got a lot stronger in the stairwell, and noise throbbed down from above— different kinds of music, voices, car crash and gunshot sounds from video games. Tut-Tut's face seemed to close up, getting hard and stony. Was he embarrassed? I wasn't sure. We went up the stairs side by side till we reached the second landing, blocked by two big guys sitting on the top step.

"Hey," said one. "The little Haitian dude."

"Got your green card, little Haitian dude?"

"Just nod."

"Yeah—we haven't got all day."

They laughed, then noticed me and went silent. I wanted so much to tell them it looked to me like they did have all day, but I didn't have the courage. But Tut-

Tut had courage, and plenty, as I already knew. He stepped into the tiny space between the men. They moved aside, not much and grudgingly, but enough so he could pass. I followed, and we kept going. As we reached the next landing, I heard one say, "Catch those sneakers?"

"Yeah," said the other, and then he called up, "Hey, little Haitian dude—you dealin', my man?"

"That how come you got a cute white girl?" said the first.

"Any dealin', you deal us in, little Haitian dude."

"Or we be dimin' you out to the INS."

More laughter. I fought the urge to run. Tut-Tut kept going at a steady, unhurried pace. We reached the third floor, went down a long windowless hall lit from above by a single bulb, all the others in the row burned out. From behind a shadowy, closed door came the sound of a woman crying and a man saying "Cry your eyes out." The next door was Tut-Tut's. He unlocked it, and we went inside.

Tut-Tut seemed to live in a single room, small and square, with a bare linoleum floor, two narrow beds, a tiny fridge, no stove—just a counter with a sink and a hot plate—and a big TV. Half the room was untidy—clothes and empty food containers all over the place; the other half was spotless, the bed made with the blanket tucked in tight and the pillow just so. Tut-Tut made a little gesture with his hand; I took it to mean "welcome."

"D-d-d-," he said. "D-dr-dr—"

"I'm good," I said. Tut-Tut was poor. I actually felt thirsty—it was so hot in the building—but I didn't want to add to his burden.

But he looked disappointed, and said, "Dr-dr-dri-drink?" Hey! He'd completed the word! He smiled. I'd never seen anything quite like it—shy, relieved, surprised, proud.

"Sure," I said. "If you're having something."

Tut-Tut opened the fridge. Inside I saw three six-packs of beer, a jar of peanut butter, two eggs, half a loaf of sliced white bread, and a large plastic bottle of Coke. Tut-Tut took out the bottle of Coke, filled two plastic glasses sporting beer company logos, and handed one to me. The occasion felt strangely formal. I clinked glasses, something I'd never initiated before. Tut-Tut clinked back. We drank. Then Tut-Tut put his glass, still mostly full, back in the fridge, and went to the neatly made bed. He crouched down, pulled out a scrolled-up sheet of paper from underneath the bed, and gave it to me.

"What's this?" I said.

"O-o-," he said. "O-op-op-op—" And came so close to saying open.

I unrolled the sheet of paper, lined paper torn from a

spiral notebook. Whoa! He'd made a pencil drawing of me. It was so good! First, no question that it was me, even though this face was much better-looking than mine, more like the face I'd see in my best dreams, if you saw your own face in dreams, which I never had. Second, this was me without my glasses. And when had Tut-Tut seen me without my glasses? Only when the power was working inside me. Was this me with the power? If so, I liked me with the power. I couldn't stop gazing at this portrait: as though it was the portrait of a stranger, and I was learning so much about her.

"Tut-Tut," I said, "I love this. You're so talen—"

At that moment, without warning, the door banged open and a man came barging in. Tut-Tut made a startled motion, almost jumped off the ground. I was pretty startled myself. The man was tall and thin, wore a studded leather jacket, and had high cheekbones a lot like Tut-Tut's. In fact, his face resembled Tut-Tut's in other ways, almost a grown-up version, although the effect was completely different. Tut-Tut had a sweet face; this guy's was mean. One other thing: I smelled booze right away.

"What the heck?" said the guy, only he didn't say "heck," and then more in the French-sounding Creole language I'd heard Tut-Tut speak that one time when the power was in him. The guy pointed once or twice at me.

Tut-Tut shook his head. "N-n-n-n-," he said. "N-n-n-n—"

"N-n-n-n-," the guy mimicked.

I'd witnessed this mimicry of Tut-Tut before, from those skateboarders, but coming from an adult, it was even more horrible.

"Hey!" I said, maybe not the smartest thing to do, but the word popped out on its own.

The guy turned to me. His eyes were bloodshot, and one of his eyelids twitched a bit. "You got something to say?"

I tried to meet his gaze but couldn't. Also my mouth had gone dry. "Please don't mimic," I said. It didn't come out with much oomph, and right away I regretted that *please*.

He took a step toward me. The room got a lot smaller, and it was small to begin with. "I say what I want," he said. His English was very good, with just a slight accent.

"But—" I began.

He held up his hand, a nicely shaped hand—kind of like Tut-Tut's, but a lot bigger, and also the tip of his index finger, from the top knuckle on, was missing. "Who are you?"

"I'm his friend."

The guy wagged his maimed finger at me. "He has no friends. He has his uncle Jean-Claude, *ki an tout*." He tapped himself on the chest. "Without me, the little retard would be living on the street. Who feeds him? Who puts the clothes on his back?"

But Tut-Tut was so skinny, and his clothes were practically rags. My voice rose; I just couldn't help it. "He's not a retard!"

Jean-Claude closed in a little more, bringing the booze cloud with him. "Look at him."

I turned to Tut-Tut. He stood motionless, his mouth slightly open, his lips moving a little, as though he were saying something. But there was no sound; and he had a thin, shiny tear track on each cheek.

"You think a retard can do this?" I said, and waved Tut-Tut's drawing at him.

Big mistake, which I knew almost in the nick of time. But not quite. Jean-Claude snatched the drawing out of my hand, barely gave it a glance, and tore it to shreds and tossed them away. Then a sound did come out of Tut-Tut's mouth, low and harsh. He charged at Jean-Claude. Jean-Claude knocked him aside with one backhanded sweep of his arm, and Tut-Tut, so light, went flying. He crashed against the wall, slid to the floor, and sat there, slumped and stunned.

I was stunned, too. And then I thought: the power. Wasn't this the kind of moment that awoke the power? I waited to feel some sign of it in my head—tingling, pressure, electricity—but I felt nothing. Why not? Where was the power now when I really needed it? Wasn't this injustice, injustice of a very cruel kind? I squeezed my eyes shut, trying my hardest to make it happen. Nothing, nada, zip, a complete waste of time, as I should have known. And there was no time to waste: when I opened my eyes I saw Jean-Claude advancing on Tut-Tut and unbuckling his belt. At the same time, Tut-Tut was reaching into his pocket.

I remembered something I'd kind of buried: *I have a knife, and I know how to use it.*

"No!" I darted past Jean-Claude, grabbed Tut-Tut's hand and pulled him to his feet. Jean-Claude tried to grab me, or Tut-Tut, or both of us, but lost his balance—maybe drunker than I'd thought—and fell. I ran to the door, hauling Tut-Tut behind, threw it open, and kept going. Behind us, Jean-Claude yelled something in Creole, the tone of it very clear.

16

The next thing I knew, we were outside. The air caught my attention, smelling so fresh and sweet for Brooklyn. Tut-Tut and I were still holding hands, but now I had the sense that he was leading me instead of me leading him. We rounded a corner, went left at the next cross street—the sign, crooked and rusty, reading Sherwood Street and came to a derelict block lined by a big fenced-in empty lot, trash-strewn and overgrown with weeds, and then a huge warehouse, dark and boarded up. An unlit alley ran alongside the warehouse. Tut-Tut led me around to the back.

"What are we—" I began, but Tut-Tut laid a finger across my lips. We walked silently behind the warehouse, the feel of his touch lingering for a moment or two, which took me by surprise, and came to a loading dock that jutted out at about chest level. Tut-Tut made a little motion, and we climbed up.

The loading dock had a big steel door, the kind that rolls down, padlocked at the bottom. Set into the big steel door was a much smaller door for people to use when they didn't need to bother with the whole rolling-up, rolling-down thing. This knobless little door—a metal plate hid the hole where the knob had been—had a window in it, covered by a plywood square. Tut-Tut reached into his pocket and pulled out a knife. Yes, he really did have a knife, something I hadn't been sure about until that moment. But this was no deadly weapon. It was short, with a small stubby blade, very dull. I recognized the type. We didn't actually have one in our kitchen, but Nonna did, and I'd seen it on our last visit to Arizona. Nonna had taught me that you use it to transfer a sliver of butter from the butter dish onto your bread plate and then do the actual spreading onto the slice of bread or roll—from which you break off a small piece at a time—with the outermost right-hand side knife of your place setting, or maybe the innermost one. The point was that, yes, Tut-Tut did pack a weapon, but it turned out to be a butter knife.

He stepped up to the window, stuck the butter knife into the crack between the plywood square and the window frame, and wiggled it back and forth. The plywood square came loose. Tut-Tut reached through the hole— there was no glass—and opened the door from the inside.

Then he put the plywood back in place, wedging it in firmly. He held the door for me. Tut-Tut probably had less of a clue than I did about what cutlery to use when, and all of Nonna's other etiquette rules, but he had old-fashioned manners just the same.

We went inside the warehouse. I got the sense of a huge empty space but couldn't see much because there was hardly any light at all, just late-afternoon murkiness leaking in here and there from windows not quite properly boarded up. Tut-Tut moved along the wall a few feet, seemed to crouch down, reaching for something. Then came the snick of a match being lit, and a moment later, Tut-Tut was beside me, a burning candle in his hand. The candlelight forced back the shadows, and I picked out details: a row of tall floor-to-ceiling pillars leading into distant shadows, pipes and ducts running up walls and crisscrossing above our heads, bare cement floor with dirt and dust everywhere, and spiderwebs, lots of them. I don't like spiders—there's something cunning about them—and stayed close to Tut-Tut as we walked along the row of pillars.

On the far side of the warehouse, we came to some kind of lift: not what I'd call an elevator, because it had no doors or walls, was just a square steel slab raised a few inches above the floor. Tut-Tut stepped onto it, motioned for me to follow.

"Where are we going?" I said, keeping my voice at whisper level.

He pointed to the ceiling. I looked up, saw a dark opening in it, about the same size and shape as the steel slab. I stepped onto it. Tut-Tut pressed a button I hadn't noticed on the wall. The steel slab gave a little shudder and then began rising, slow and silent. We rose, taking the light with us, leaving darkness below.

In a moment or two, we passed through the opening in the ceiling. The lift reached floor level and came to a stop. We were in a room, small enough that Tut-Tut's candle illuminated just about everything in it: a desk, two swivel chairs, some rolled-up blankets, a wide-plank wooden floor. But I didn't really take in any of that at first; what grabbed my attention were the pictures spray-painted on the walls: parrots, flowers, butterflies, all in Tut-Tut's style. And there was Tut-Tut's tag, *vudu,* in purple. Plus some faces: Tut-Tut himself, his uncle Jean-Claude, a man and a woman, each with their eyes closed. The woman shared Tut-Tut and Jean-Claude's high-cheekbone look; the man's face seemed gentle and kind, although with his eyes closed, it was hard to be sure.

I took a guess. "Is that your mother?"

Tut-Tut nodded.

And the kindly man with the closed eyes? "Your father?"

Tut-Tut nodded again.

"Are they still in Haiti?" I said.

Tut-Tut shook his head, one curt movement.

"Oh," I said. So what was the implication of that, exactly? I glanced again at those two closed-eye portraits.

Meanwhile Tut-Tut was dripping some molten wax on the desktop. He stuck the candle in it, sat in one of the swivel chairs, opened a desk drawer, and took out a spiral notebook and a pencil. It began to hit me, maybe somewhat late, that this room was Tut-Tut's private office, and maybe, given those rolled-up blankets, his shelter, too.

"How did you find this place?" I asked.

Tut-Tut shrugged, like it was a long story, or not important, or maybe both. Then he opened the notebook to a blank page and started drawing.

A scene began to take shape: flat, empty ocean with a big sun overhead; a beat-up sailboat crowded with people, all of them sketched so quickly, all with closed eyes, except for one small figure in the bow. His eyes were open, and even though only pencil marks, were amazingly like the real eyes I was seeing now. Then came another scene: empty ocean, but now very rough, with towering waves and rain pelting down; no sailboat, no people. Tut-Tut opened the drawer again, took out a pencil sharpener—PROPERTY OF NYC BOARD OF EDUCA-

TION, it said on the side—and sharpened the pencil. He turned back to that rough, empty ocean and, with a few quick strokes, added a broken mast floating in the water, and the small figure clinging to it. You couldn't see his face, just his hands and his modified dreads.

"Oh, my God," I said.

Tut-Tut made that little shrug again. Then he tore the page from the notebook and held it to the flame. It caught fire, shining brightly on his face, very solemn at that moment. He dropped the burning paper into a metal wastebasket beside the desk, where it quickly turned to ash.

We walked back to Tut-Tut's apartment. "Sure it's okay?" I said.

Tut-Tut nodded. Maybe there was some sort of routine going on and he knew that Jean-Claude would be gone now, or passed out, or in a different mood.

"Bye," I said.

"B-b-b-b-," said Tut-Tut.

Half an hour later, I was back home. "Hi! I'm back!"

Silence. I was headed for the fridge when my phone rang.

"Robbie?" It was my mom.

"Hi."

"Are you at home?"

"Yeah."

I could feel her relax a bit, even though she hadn't made a sound. "What's Pendleton up to?"

I glanced around, spotted him under the kitchen table. "Sleeping."

"Can you take him for a walk?"

"Okay."

"Thanks, honey. I'll be another hour or so."

"Working on the New Brooklyn Redevelopment Project?"

"No." There was a pause. "Why do you ask that?"

"I don't know, Mom. But it's pretty bad, right?"

"Bad? In what way?"

"The rich taking from the poor," I said. "That way."

"It's not so simple," Mom said. "Let's talk about it when I get home."

I had a snack—chips and salsa washed down with lemonade, a great combo—and turned to Pendleton. "Ready for your walk?"

But he wasn't.

"Come on, Pendleton, don't make this hard."

Pendleton made it hard. He wriggled farther back under the table, twisted his head away when I crawled under with the leash, dug in his heels when I got it attached and tried to drag him out.

"How about a treat?" I said, which was where I should

have started. In moments, we were on the street, Pendleton right beside me, pressing his nose against the pocket that held the biscuit. "First do what you're supposed to do," I said. In my other pocket, I had the plastic bag for dealing with what Pendleton was supposed to do once he'd done it. "Could be worse, Pendleton," I told him. "Like if we had to walk pet elephants." He showed no reaction, instead cowered against a building to let a Chihuahua pass by.

"Robbie?"

I turned. "Silas?"

"Hi," he said. Silas wore a tight red watch cap that emphasized the roundness of his face and made him hard to recognize. "Is that your dog?"

"Yeah."

"Is he safe?"

"Safe?"

"I got bitten by a dog once."

"You won't get bitten by Pendleton. You can pat him if you like."

"That's all right," he said. "What are you doing here, anyway?"

"It's my neighborhood, Silas. What's your excuse?"

He glanced around. "I'm doing some research," he said, lowering his voice.

"Into what?"

174

He reached into his jacket, one of those padded Michelin-man-type jackets, and took out a bundle of printouts. "I'm mapping all the venues."

"What does that mean?"

"Of the people getting kicked out of their places by Sheldon Gunn."

"Hey! You found that list from Sheldon Gunn Is a Monster?"

"Not exactly. It's a little more complicated. I tracked down this server in Finland, and he and I—or it might have been a she—tweaked some code from these other people in China, hidden in a steganographic app, actually, that—"

"Silas? I'm convinced. But the point is you've got the list?"

"Right here," he said, waving the sheaf of papers, a pleased smile on his face, although a bit distracting on account of the braces on his teeth, the most prominent I'd ever seen. And in that moment of distraction, with me staring at his teeth and him staring at me staring, he lost his grip on the papers. They scattered like cards in Fifty-two Pickup and then the wind rose and scattered them some more.

Silas and I went hurrying after them, but I got tangled up in Pendleton's leash right away. "Pendleton! For God's sake!" He whimpered. What was the point of getting mad at Pendleton? I unlooped myself from the leash, saw Silas scurrying along the gutter, scooping up papers. He slipped on a grating, almost fell, and lost one or two. They came drifting back toward me. I snatched one right out of the air. The other one veered up onto the sidewalk and miraculously stayed still. I bent down to take the stupid thing, but a man stepped on it first. I didn't see the whole man, just his shoe—a gleaming black shoe, the leather of the soft, expensive kind. I glanced up, took in a fancy dark topcoat, the perfect knot of a silk tie, and finally a face with perfectly symmetrical features, a square-jawed face that seemed a bit familiar, but I didn't know why until I noticed the hair—very light, almost platinum—and worn short. I'd seen this man before, on a motorcycle outside Heinz Mott's apartment. But way more surprising than that was the fact that my mom was standing beside him.

"Robbie?" she said.

"Uh, hi, Mom."

The man gazed down at me, his eyes silvery blue, unreadable. I noticed he was carrying a briefcase, but a real battered and scruffy one that didn't seem to match the rest of his getup.

"What are you doing?" my mom said.

"Taking Pendleton for a walk, like you said," I told her. At the same time I was trying to tug the sheet of paper out from under the man's foot, and he wasn't helping in the least.

And now Silas was coming back, in an ungainly sort of trot. "Got most of them—" he began, and then noticed the confusing scene and went quiet. My mom turned to him, looking puzzled.

"Mom, Silas," I said, not knowing what else to do. "Silas, Mom."

And I'd barely got through the introductions when—another surprise—the man stooped down quickly and smoothly and picked up the sheet of paper himself.

"Um," I said, and started to get up, bracing myself with one hand on Pendleton. With the other, I reached for the paper, but the man leaned back, keeping it out of my reach, moving it toward reading level.

"Egil," my mom began, "this is my daughter, Robbie. Robbie, this is Egil Borg, a colleague of—"

Egil Borg? The signer of those threatening letters to Mr. Nok and Heinz Mott? *Wham!* The fastest yet—and strongest, too—the power came zooming back. Was there a headache? Electric ball? Vision change? Maybe all those things, but I was only aware of the silver heart fluttering on my wrist and then a surge down my arm into my hand, the hand in contact with Pendleton's soft shoulder.

That soft shoulder hardened instantly—I felt it under

my hand—hardened and bunched with muscle. Then Pendleton snarled, a savage and terrifying sound, impossible that it could be coming from him. Not only that, but he was suddenly rising up, his mouth wide open, teeth exposed, saliva dripping all over the place.

"Pendleton!" I cried, and so did my mom. But too late. Pendleton sprang at Egil Borg, a pretty big guy, and knocked him down like he was a cardboard cutout. Pendleton surged forward and stood over him, barking his head off, those teeth—suddenly so sharp-looking—inches from Egil Borg's face. I took advantage of the situation to grab the paper from his hand and tuck it away.

"Maybe I should be going," said Silas.

"Good idea," I told him.

17

eanwhile Pendleton—this new Pendleton, transformed by the power—was still straddling my mom's colleague, Egil Borg, barking and snarling. Whenever Borg tried to wriggle away, Pendleton lowered his head and barked and snarled louder.

"Pendleton!" Mom screamed. She grabbed his leash and pulled with all her strength, not budging Pendleton an inch. I went forward to help her, reached out for Pendleton's collar. Somehow he'd gotten it all twisted around so the metal tag was at the back, and that was what my hand closed around.

Zap! A shock hit me, passed through my hand, into my wrist. The silver heart fluttered again and then went still. So did Pendleton. He stopped barking and snarling and after a few seconds raised his head and looked kind of confused. Then he rolled over and lay on the sidewalk, all four paws in the air, his posture when he wanted his stomach scratched.

"Egil," my mom said. "Are you all right? I'm so sorry. I don't know what got into him." She extended her hand to help him up. Borg pushed her hand away and rose by himself. "He's never done anything remotely like this. Pendleton's a big pussycat, afraid of his own shadow."

"Somehow I missed that," Borg said, brushing himself off. A little crowd had gathered. He glared at them with his ice-blue eyes, and they all moved on.

"No, really," Mom said. "This is so out of character." She turned to me. "Did anything happen to him on the walk, Robbie?"

"No."

Mom looked around. "Where's that friend of yours?"

"He went home."

"Did he tease Pendleton?"

"No, Mom."

"What was his name again?"

"Silas," said Borg before I could reply.

"I don't think you've mentioned him before," my mom said.

"Mom. He didn't do anything to Pendleton."

She turned to me, which is why she couldn't have seen Borg picking up his briefcase, now a little more battered. For a microsecond the briefcase opened up, just a fraction of an inch, but I glimpsed money in there, stacked in bundles. Borg clamped it shut, real quick, and shifted the keys of the combination lock.

"Then what got into him?" Mom was saying. "I don't understand."

The power, this very flaky power, had suddenly entered Pendleton and just as suddenly vanished. That was the answer, but was this the time to cough it up? Would there ever be that time? I gazed down at Pendleton, still on his back but now wriggling around, which is what he did when people didn't pick up on the stomach-scratching hint fast enough.

Mom shook her head, totally puzzled. "Egil, I feel terrible about this. Our place is just down the block—why don't you come over? I could sew on that button, or—"

Borg glanced down at the front of his coat, noticed the dangling button. He ripped it off and tossed it in the street. "I'm already running late." His gaze went to me, back to Mom. "See you tomorrow." He turned and strode away.

"Oh, my God," my mom said.

"Is it that big a deal, Mom? He didn't get hurt."

My mom's voice rose. "You don't understand. And this new friend of yours—is he the one who gave you that bracelet, by the way?"

"Bracelet?"

She pointed. "On your wrist."

"Oh, right. No, Mom."

"It wasn't him?"

I shook my head.

Mom paused, maybe giving me a chance to cough up the name. Then, when I kept my mouth shut, she went on, "Well, he looked pretty shifty to me. I can't believe he had nothing to do with—"

"Shifty?" My voice rose, too. "Silas isn't shifty." But even as I said that, a quiet countervoice inside me was asking, *Really? It's not a bit shifty to be hacking on the net and inventing software to open combination locks?* I took the edge off my tone and said, "He didn't do anything to Pendleton—I promise."

Mom took a deep breath. "Okay," she said. "I believe you." Promises were very important to my mom. She gazed down at Pendleton; he'd stopped writhing around, was now just waiting patiently. "It's such unbelievably bad luck. Why of all people . . ."

"Egil Borg?"

She nodded. "He was on my train tonight—that's why we were walking together."

"Does he live near here?"

Mom shook her head. "He lives somewhere in Connecticut, but he was meeting some people for dinner. I hardly know him—and want to keep it that way."

"Why?"

"It's complicated," Mom said.

An expression I was hearing too much, all of a sudden. "Try me," I said.

"Egil is a special kind of lawyer."

"Is he one of the partners?"

"Not officially. His exact financial relationship with the firm is a mystery, at least to me."

I told her about the money in the briefcase.

She blinked, a long, slow blink she sometimes did when hearing things she didn't like. "I suppose it shouldn't be unexpected. Egil is a fixer."

"What does that mean?"

"Maybe 'troubleshooter' is a better expression. One of the partners got into an accident on Long Island a few years ago, for example, and Egil smoothed it all out."

"A drunk-driving accident?"

"Don't know the details," Mom said, "and I don't really want to know."

That disappointed me. I had no right to be disappointed by my mom—she was a great mother—but I felt disappointment all the same.

Did she see it on my face? She touched my shoulder and said, "This is a big city, Robbie, and very hard in some ways."

"I know, Mom."

"You do?" She looked surprised, then stepped forward and gave me a hug. Pendleton started whining right away; he disliked shows of affection that didn't involve him. I bent down and scratched his stupid stomach. He rolled over and got up. We headed for home, met the Chihuahua coming the other way. Pendleton cringed against a wall.

Back at home, I sat at my desk, working on a problem: *The grocery store parking lot will hold 1,000 vehicles* (so we were not in Brooklyn; I knew that right away), *and 2/5 of the parking spaces are for cars. When you go to buy groceries* (Hey! Would I own a car one day? What would be a good choice? I realized I knew practically nothing about cars.), *there are 200 cars and some trucks in the parking lot, which is 3/4 full. How many trucks are there?* I gazed at that for a while, then turned to the scrap of paper I'd rescued from Egil Borg. It was a list of names and addresses, none of which I recognized except for Your Thai. A few of them were printed in red, but not Your Thai.

My phone rang. It was Silas.

"I thought your dog was supposed to be gentle," he said.

"He is."

"Yeah? Then what got into him?"

"Take a guess."

"He ate something spicy?"

"Silas. Do you attack people if you eat something spicy?"

"Why would I? I like spicy."

"So does Pendleton." Pendleton had never met a food product he didn't like. I got up, closed my door. "What got into him was the power."

"Wow. It can jump species?"

"I just know it can jump to Pendleton," I said. "I've got one of your pages. What does it mean if something's in red?"

"I've been wondering about that. Right now I'm working on this map of everybody getting pushed out by Sheldon Gunn."

"And?"

"And there are so many! It's like he's taking over the whole of Brooklyn."

"What for?"

"What for?" said Silas. "Don't you play any video games?"

"No."

"It's so he can win. Don't you—"

In the background, I heard a woman say, "What are you talking about, Silas?"

"Video games, Mom," he said. And then to me: "Gotta go." *Click.*

I wrote down *550 trucks,* a number that just jumped into my head.

• • •

That night sirens woke me up, real loud sirens racing down our street, one after another. I got out of bed and went into the hall. Mom and Dad were already there, gazing out the window.

"What's going on?" I said.

"Must be a fire somewhere nearby," my dad said.

I squeezed in between them, checked down at the street. Firefighters were hauling a hose toward a hydrant, and there were already spectators, some in winter jackets and pajama bottoms.

"I should really see this," Dad said.

My mom gave him a funny look.

"I want to go, too," I said.

"Get back to bed," she told me.

"Come on, Mom. How can I sleep with all the noise?"

"She's right," Dad said. "Let's all go."

Mom shook her head. "Too ghoulish," she said.

So just my dad and I went, but fully dressed. "Are we pajamas-on-the-street kind of people?" my dad said, I guess teaching me that we weren't. We followed the hose down the block and around the corner, and there, on the far side of the street, a three- or four-story row house was on fire, flames roaring up to the sky and firefighters on ladders and on the ground spraying water in jets that looked kind of puny.

"Hey," said my dad, "I love that building."

I'd never noticed it before. The building seemed like lots of others around, maybe narrower than most. "What's special about it?"

"It's a landmark building," he said, "one of the only original Federalist examples in the neighborhood."

"What does landmark mean?"

"The owner can't make any important changes—it has to be preserved."

But it was much too late for that. As we watched, a whole big wall collapsed, flinging fiery debris into the night. The firefighters shouted for everyone to get back, and as we withdrew, I took notice of some of the people around me.

Such as: a man and a woman in tears, both in long coats and barefoot. She held a painting of some flowers, he held her, and they both gazed at the fire, tears streaming down their faces.

And: way at the back, leaning against the shuttered wall of a bodega, a little long-nosed guy who also couldn't take his eyes off the fire. But no tears from him: he looked fascinated and kind of excited. Was there a word for people who got excited by fires? I couldn't think of it at the moment, and was about to turn away from the guy when I saw that he had a briefcase in his hand; in his hand, but also resting on a stoop. There was something familiar about that briefcase. I sidled a little closer, took a better look. Yes, a battered and scuffed-up briefcase, just like the one Egil Borg had been carrying. In fact, so much like it that—

The power hit me. *Hit* was the wrong word this time, and there was certainly no zap. Now the power seemed to come slowly and gently, trailing the slightest headache, hardly worthy of the name of pain. I had a second or two to take off my glasses and stick them safely in my pocket before my vision changed.

I kept my eyes on the long-nosed guy and waited. The pressure built behind my eyes and then the red-gold beam flashed out, invisible to everyone but me. The beam homed in on the briefcase, specifically striking the two ends of the handle. Then came two tiny sparks. The briefcase wobbled slightly on the stoop, but remained upright; the long-nosed guy didn't feel the movement because the briefcase was no longer connected to the handle, and he didn't feel a change in the weight because he hadn't been bearing any of it.

I glanced at my dad—he was writing in his notebook—and sidled over some more. At that moment, there was an enormous *KA-BOOM,* and a big chunk of the roof exploded high into the air, sparks shooting all over the place. The long-nosed guy, still holding the severed handle, got this ecstatic look on his face, the fire shining in his eyes. I swiped the briefcase in one smooth move, tucked it under the back of my jacket and partly beneath my belt, and quickly made my way through the crowd to my dad's side.

"I'm ready to go home," I said.

"Me too—it's just as I would have imagined," my dad said. We walked off. "Where are your glasses, by the way?"

"Oh, yeah," I said, taking them out of my pocket and putting them back on. But the power still lingered in me, so my vision actually got blurry.

"You'll have contacts before you know it," my dad said. "Just be patient."

"Okay, Dad."

18

Back in my room, vision returned to normal, sirens no longer sounding, the night pretty quiet, and Mom and Dad asleep, I switched on my bedside light and took the briefcase out from under my bed. It was one of those rectangular, hard-bodied ones, with two brass fasteners that released when you dialed the right combination. The combination lock was made of brass, just a flat piece between the fasteners with four numbers showing—at the moment, 8657. I tried 1111, just in case Egil Borg or the long-nosed guy thought no one would be that stupid, and when that didn't work, I clicked through 9999 and then my birthday, followed by a bunch of random numbers. Nada. Even if I could cut through the hard body with a kitchen knife, it meant going downstairs in the middle of the night, clattering around in the knife drawer, and maybe waking someone and leading to a scene that wouldn't be good. I shoved the briefcase under my bed, switched off my light, and lay sleepless for a while. Then I thought, *Combination lock!* And closed my eyes.

I saw Ashanti at basketball the next day. She and her mother—her father was on a shoot in LA—had slept right through the fire, hadn't heard a thing.

"How is that possible?" I said.

"My mother's a real light sleeper, so we had the place soundproofed," Ashanti said. "We even have quadruple-paned windows. It's like living in . . ." She searched for a word.

The country? I thought. A tomb? Before Ashanti came up with whatever it was, Ms. Kleinberg blew her whistle and yelled, "What are you two gossiping about? Five laps."

We ran around the gym five times while the rest of the team also ran, but through this maze of cones and dribbling basketballs at the same time, a drill that always ended in chaos.

"Stay low," Ms. Kleinberg called to all the dribblers. "What do you have knees for?"

Balls began bouncing all over the place, and Ms. Kleinberg had no more time for Ashanti and me. While we ran, I told Ashanti all about Egil Borg, the long-nosed guy, the briefcase.

"Borg's the one who wrote that threatening letter to Heinz Mott?" she said.

"Yeah."

"You think he paid the long-nosed guy to set the fire?"

"He's the fixer," I told her. "My mom said a fixer is a—"

"I know what a fixer is," Ashanti said. I suppose that was a strange thing about Ashanti, the way she could snap at you unexpectedly; even stranger was the fact that I was starting to like it. "The question," she went on, "is whether Silas is ready with his combo-busting app."

"I was thinking the same thing," I said.

"We need to get together," Ashanti said. "You, me, Silas, briefcase."

"Yeah, but where?"

"Your place after school?"

I shook my head. "My dad might be there. Or he could come back any time. How about your place?"

"Yeah, right," said Ashanti.

"Silas's?"

"Nope—his big brother's back."

"Silas has a brother?"

"Thaddeus. He's some kind of genius."

"Home from college?"

"Rehab," Ashanti said. We ran a few more steps,

came to the scorer's table, where we'd started. "That's five," Ashanti said. We stopped running, huffed and puffed a bit, hands on hips. "So where?" Ashanti said.

"I've got an idea," I said.

"Girls?" Ms. Kleinberg called over. "That's only four."

We began running again.

"How about we make it six?" Ms. Kleinberg said. "Just in case there was anything on purpose about that miscount."

We met on Saturday at Tut-Tut's office inside the Sherwood Street warehouse, Tut-Tut, Silas, Ashanti, me. I'd told my dad—Mom had to work—that I was hanging with Ashanti, and she'd told her mom she was hanging with me. All totally true, depending on the precise legal meaning of "hanging with." Silas had told his brother he was doing some research, and Tut-Tut had no one to tell, unless you included Jean-Claude.

Tut-Tut had found a space heater from somewhere, so it was nice and warm. He also produced two more swivel chairs. We sat around the desk like businessmen.

"Wow," said Silas. "A real clubhouse."

Ashanti turned to him. "How old are you?" she said.

"Thirteen-point-two-five."

"Then act it."

Tut-Tut laughed. Had I ever heard him laugh before? He had a great laugh, the contagious kind. Soon we were all laughing. Tut-Tut opened the desk drawer, took out his can of purple paint, rolled his swivel chair to the wall, hopped up on it, and above all the faces sprayed *HQ* in his tagging style, a sort of warping, ballooning thing, almost like the letters might move around at any moment.

"Exactly," said Ashanti. "This is headquarters."

I had an odd thought: *Tut-Tut is a great communicator.*

Now," said Ashanti, "what are we going to call ourselves?"

"The Brooklyn Krewe?" said Silas. "You know, with a *K,* like the parades? Mardi Gras? New Orleans, anybody?"

Ashanti's eyes shifted to him.

"Maybe a little too . . . um?" Silas said.

We sat in silence, swiveling a bit from time to time.

"Let's think of what we're trying to do," I said.

Tut-Tut nodded. The others nodded.

"The Sheldon Gunn Is a Monster Boys?" Silas said. He glanced around the desk. "And Girls?"

Tut-Tut laughed again. Yes, a lovely laugh, with no hesitation or effort. On the other hand, wasn't laughter, with that repeated ha-ha-ha, kind of like stuttering? I got the feeling that was the sort of idea my dad might have had at a moment like this, and pushed it aside.

"What?" said Silas. "No one likes it? Let's vote."

We ignored him.

"How about the New Brooklyn Redevelopment Anti-Project," Ashanti said.

"Hey," I said.

Silas jumped up. He was turning out to be more excitable than I'd first thought. "That's catchier than mine?"

Ashanti glared at him, but the glare faded quickly. "Maybe not," she said.

We went back to sitting and swiveling. Tut-Tut doodled with a pencil on a scrap of paper. At first I couldn't make out what it was, and then I did: my bracelet from all sorts of different angles.

"But," said Ashanti after a while, "is that what we're doing really, stopping the project?"

"What else?" said Silas. "He's kicking people onto the street."

"We can't let him," I said.

"No," said Ashanti. "But I'm talking about our motto."

"What's our motto?" Silas said.

"Something wrong with your memory?" Ashanti said. "Robbing from the rich, giving to the poor? Ring a bell?"

Tut-Tut's eyes opened wide.

"Do you like that motto?" I said.

"Y-y-ye-ye-," said Tut-Tut, getting so close to yeah

that we all yelled out "yeah!" together. Then we were all laughing again, like this tight little band . . . a band, in fact, of outlaws.

"Hey!" I said. "How about the Outlaws?"

"Cool," said Ashanti.

"Dyn-o-mite," said Silas.

"Y-y-ye-ye—"

"So we're agreed?" I said. "The Outlaws?"

"I don't know," said Ashanti. "Shouldn't your name be in there somewhere?"

"Huh?" I said.

"The power started with you," she said. "Maybe it even comes from you."

"Oh, no," I said. "It's in the bracelet." But was I sure about that? No.

"Yeah?" Ashanti said. "Then how come the bracelet wants to be on your wrist and nobody else's?"

"Like it's for a meant-to-be reason—Ms. Robyn Forester?" Silas said.

"What are you talking about?" Ashanti said.

"Forester?" said Silas. "Robin Hood? I mean, how obvious can you get?"

"Zip it," Ashanti said.

Silas reddened, a strange look on his particular face, with the freckles actually getting lighter. "Maybe more surreal, when you come down to it," he said.

Tut-Tut raised his hands, pretended to shoot an arrow at Silas. Ashanti gave him a long look, possibly starting to realize how smart Tut-Tut was, something I already knew.

"Okay, Silas," she said, "How about this? The Outlaws of Sherwood Street."

Perfect.

Ashanti laid her hand on the desk. Silas laid his on top of hers, then Tut-Tut, then me. Four hands, very different, but there was something powerful, seeing them stacked up like that.

"Aren't we leaving someone out?" Silas said.

"Who would that be?" said Ashanti.

"Pendleton's paw should be in here somewhere," Silas told her.

"Can we rely on Pendleton, Robbie?" Ashanti said.

Rely on Pendleton? That didn't compute in any way. "The big problem is we can't even really rely on the power," I said.

"What power?" Silas said. "I don't have it."

"Yeah, you do," I said. "When you handed me that sheet of paper, the one about Heinz Mott, and it burst into flames? You felt an electric ball thing in your head, right?"

"Yeah."

"Then you've got the power."

"But I can't do anything! You've got the laser, and Ashanti can fly, for God's sake—"

"It's more like soaring," Ashanti said.

"But what can I do?" Silas said. "Or Tut-Tut, for that matter?"

Tut-Tut frowned, like he'd just been insulted. "I c-c-c-c—"

"When the power's in him, he talks better than all of us put together," I said.

"Say what?" said Silas.

Ashanti separated Silas's hand from the others and gave it a smack.

"Ow," he said.

"My guess," I said, "is that Silas's power is still out there somewhere."

"But when will I get it?" Silas said. He glanced at Ashanti, and even though she wasn't watching him, stuck his hands in his pockets, real quick.

"The point is," I said, "what have you got for us today?"

"Huh?"

"The app, Silas. Didn't you tell Ashanti it was ready?"

"The one-point-oh is ready," Silas said. He wagged his finger. "That's an important caveat."

"Keep it to yourself," Ashanti said.

I laid the briefcase on the table.

Silas peered at it. "Where's the combination lock?"

"Right there," I said, pointing. "Those thingies."

"But I've been working on the other kind," Silas said. "You know—that hang on lockers and stuff."

"A combination lock is a combination lock," Ashanti said. "You're wasting time."

Silas took out his cell phone, pressed a button or two, then pointed it at the briefcase. He checked the screen and smiled that huge metallic smile of his. "Eureka moment, everybody," he said, and showed us the screen. Four numbers: 7, 3, 9, 1.

"Who wants to do the honors?" Silas said. When no one spoke up in the next microsecond, he went on: "How about the inventor himself?"

The inventor himself reached out and clicked through the numbers on all four dials until they came up 7391. "And presto," he said. The two brass snaps stayed where they were. He frowned, pressed some more buttons on the phone, again pointed it at the briefcase, and checked the screen. "These are the right numbers."

"Maybe give the briefcase a little tap," I said.

"You call that science?" said Silas. He turned all the dials, set them back at 7391. Nada.

"Hmm," he said. "Wonder if . . ." He pressed more buttons. The space heater made a sudden sizzling sound and then cut off. "Hmm" Silas said again. He repeated the whole button-pressing, phone-pointing routine again. A beeping sound came from the direction of the elevator and then it shuddered and started going down. We all jumped up, hurried to what was now just a hole in the HQ floor, and watched the elevator until it touched down on the warehouse floor below—quite far below, I realized for the first time.

"We could hang from each other," Silas said, "kind of a chain with the . . ." He felt our gazes and went silent.

A moment or two later, the elevator started back up. It reached our level, shuddered again, and stayed put.

We returned to the desk.

"Nothing to be alarmed about," Silas said. "Quite typical for a one-point-oh version. Give me a few days to work out the bugs and—"

Tut-Tut tapped the side of the briefcase, not very hard. It sprang open.

E mpty?" Ashanti said. "How can it be empty?" She turned to me. "I thought you said—"

"But it was," I said, voice rising, heart sinking. "It was full of money. Stacks and stacks."

Ashanti turned the briefcase upside down and shook it. No money fell out, not a single stupid bill. Then all eyes were on me. Wasn't I supposed to be some sort of leader? Not that I'd ever wanted to be a leader—class president, team captain, any of that. I was happy not being a leader. But without pushing or scheming to be the leader, I'd kind of fallen into the role and, in my very first act, blown the whole thing.

My instinct was to apologize to everybody, tell them I didn't want to be the leader, withdraw into the background. Were instincts usually right? Go with your gut: that was what my dad always said. Check everything and then check it again: that was my mom. On this one, I went with her.

"I saw what I saw," I said, keeping my head up.

There was a pause. Then Ashanti said, "I believe you."

Silas bit his lip, gazed at the ceiling, scratched the side of his nose, and then nodded.

Tut-Tut took the briefcase and felt around inside, like he believed me so much that the money had to be there, despite what we'd seen with our own eyes. Suddenly his hand went still. The rest of us leaned closer. He'd found a very narrow zipper in the briefcase lining. Now he pulled it open, revealing a tiny compartment. And in the compartment: a folded-up sheet of paper. Tut-Tut unfolded it and laid it on the desk.

It was a handwritten list of surnames, fifteen or twenty, the top one being Schleck. I scanned the names, recognized none.

"What's this all about?" Ashanti said.

Silas reached into his jacket, pulled out a big sheaf of papers, tire tracks visible on the top one, meaning these had to be the papers that had gotten away from him out on the street. He started riffling through them, glancing once or twice at the list from the briefcase. I could feel Ashanti's growing impatience, foresaw Silas losing his grip on the papers once more, and held up my finger to keep her quiet. Somewhat to my surprise, she remained silent.

"Any thumbtacks?" Silas said.

Tut-Tut found a box of thumbtacks. Silas went to one of the blank walls and began tacking up some of his papers, which turned out to be map printouts. He arranged them, rearranged them, and eventually we were looking at a map of the entire borough.

"Voilà," he said, stepping back. "Brooklyn." He stood there as though waiting for applause. When none came, he went on, "See where I've made little red circles? Each one is an address from the Monster blog, which no longer exists except at the end of one tiny trail I happened to track down in deepest cyberspace." The reality of this was Silas alone at the computer in his bedroom until all hours, but at that moment I understood it was like a real expedition in the wild to him, and I caught some of his excitement.

"Now," he said, picking up more papers from the desk and passing them around, "here's a whole bunch of names that Heinz Mott had in a separate file. I've started matching them up to the addresses. For example, Your Thai is right here"—he jabbed at the map—"and here's the place that burned down the other night, and the name of the people who go with it, which happens to be"—he checked a sheet that Tut-Tut was examining—"Tim and Maria Schleck."

"Schleck?" I said.

"Correck," said Silas.

Silas had a way of making your eyes roll, which mine and Ashanti's were doing, but Tut-Tut was laughing one of his delighted laughs.

"But Schleck is the first name on the list," I said.

We all checked the list Tut-Tut had found in the briefcase: *Schleck*.

"So, therefore?" Ashanti said.

"All we know is that the Schleck address went up in flames," I said. I thought of the man and woman in tears—Tim and Maria?—both in long coats and bare-foot, tears streaming down their faces. "What's the next name on the list?" I asked.

"Rewind Enterprises," Ashanti replied.

"What's that?" I said.

"No clue," she told me.

"But," said Silas, turning to the map, "it's right here." He pointed to a little red circle.

"Hey," said Ashanti. "That's just two blocks away." Everybody jumped up.

REWIND, read the sign. SATISFYING ALL YOUR VINYL NEEDS SINCE 1963.

We stood outside this tiny hole-in-the-wall store with no display windows and a glass door so dusty you couldn't see inside.

"What's vinyl?" I said, pretty sure this was not the kind of place we should be entering.

"Short for vinyl chloride," Silas said.

"Much obliged," I said.

Silas did his turning-red thing and added, "A kind of plastic. They used to make records out of it."

"My grandfather has a whole collection," said Ashanti.

Then came a big surprise. Tut-Tut opened his mouth and sang, "Home, home on the range, where the deer and the antelope play; Where seldom is heard a discouraging word, and the skies are not cloudy all day."

Tut-Tut could sing? Sing without the slightest hint of stuttering? And hit every note, besides?

"You can sing?" I said. "You've been able to sing all this time?"

"Y-y-y-ye-ye-," he said.

Silas snapped his fingers—a snap, since he was wearing gloves, that made no sound. "Wait a minute," he said. "All you've got to do is sing whatever it is you want to say."

Tut-Tut shook his head.

"Like if you want to say, 'Another chocolate chip cookie for me,' all you'd have to do is sing it."

Tut-Tut kept shaking his head, but Silas didn't seem to notice.

"Like this," he said, and sang, "Another chocolate chip cookie for me," in a grating voice, hitting none of the notes. "Or, suppose you wanted to explain vinyl. Vinyl, vinyl," he sang, even more horribly than before, "I have no idea what rhymes with vi—"

The door to Rewind flew open and an angry man glared out. "What's going on?"

"Um," we said, "uh."

"Beat it or I'll call the cops," he said.

He was bald on top, but had extremely long fringe hair, mostly gray, the back part tied in a ponytail that reached practically to his waist, the side parts just sort of hanging there, untamed and frizzy. My dad said there were maybe three hippies left in Brooklyn. This had to be one of them.

He looked us over. "Bunch of outlaws," he said.

"Outlaws?" I said. How could anyone know? We'd just finished picking the name.

"Stealin' music off the net," the hippie said. "What else do you call it?"

I'd never done that, not once. Paying for content was one of my dad's strictest rules. "We're not outlaws," I said.

"Not in that sense," added Silas.

Ashanti gave him a hard poke in the ribs.

"Huh?" said the hippie.

"Ooof," said Silas. And, "Ow."

This wasn't going well, and the hippie's eyes were getting narrower and narrower.

"We don't want to steal anything," I said.

"Meaning you want to buy?"

"Well, look around, anyway," I said.

He gazed down at me for a moment or two, then stepped aside. We filed in. It smelled very musty inside Rewind. Two long rows of record racks disappeared into dim murkiness at the rear of the store, and colorful album covers hung from the ceiling. We all found ourselves eyeing one of them, mostly because it hung so low we couldn't get by without giving it a little push, and the situation seemed too delicate for that.

The hippie noticed what we were looking at and said, "Interested in *Sergeant Pepper's Lonely Hearts Club Band*?"

"What are some of their songs?" Silas said.

A perfectly reasonable question from my point of view, but it reignited the hippie's temper. "Get out, all of you. Go, go, go." He made shooing motions with his hands, wafting some pretty bad BO our way.

"What's wrong?" I said.

"What's wrong?" he said, his voice rising. "The state of civilization—how about we start right there? You think the persecution of vinyl is just an isolated event?"

"Persecution of vinyl?" I was lost.

"Nothing exists in a vacuum," he said. "Don't you even know that? We're headed down the toilet on golden surfboards! Get it through your ridiculous twenty-first-century heads. The music's over! Turn out the lights!"

Sweat had broken out on the hippie's forehead, and

he didn't look well. As for what he was talking about, I could only guess. A wild guess, maybe, but I went with it. "You're upset about the New Brooklyn Redevelopment Project, right?"

He went still, lost all the color in his face. His lips, thin and cracked, started twitching. "Who—who are you?" he said, backing away and striking the hanging album cover, which started twirling. "What do you want?"

"Nothing," I said.

"Information," said Ashanti.

He raised his hands, palms out. "Information?" His fingers were trembling.

"For our school project," Silas said.

"Right," I said. "School project."

"On vinyl," Silas said.

This time I poked him myself. "It's on the New Brooklyn Redevelopment Project."

"For or against?" the hippie said.

"Huh?"

"You heard me—are you for or against?"

"Against," I said.

"Y-y-ye-," said Tut-Tut, so close to *yeah* that the hippie didn't notice anything about how he talked.

"Totally," said Ashanti.

"I second the emotion," said Silas. Was there any point in poking him again? I decided not.

Meanwhile the hippie was saying, "At least that's one

thing you've got right." He smacked his fist into his open hand. "The bastards!"

"Mr., uh," I began.

"Call me Bowlman," the hippie said. "Everyone does."

"Well, Mr. Bowlman, what is—"

"Just Bowlman," he said. "No mister. I despise mister."

"Er, Bowlman," I said, "why do you call them bastards?"

"Because you're just kids and I don't want to say the words I really mean in front of young ears."

"We can take it," Silas said.

"Yeah?" said Bowlman, and he let loose a big, long string of bad words, one or two completely new to me, at least in the combinations Bowlman used.

"So, uh, getting back to how come you feel that way," I said, "why don't—"

"How come I feel this way? Because I'm a human being is why! And they're bloodsuckers. Year two on a ten-year lease, black and white, but their lawyers found some stupid little mistake and got the whole thing torn up, and now they tripled the rent. Tripled!"

"The lawyers for the New Brooklyn Redevelopment Project?" I said.

"Parasites on the bloodsucker! And their hit man, Borg—don't get me started on him!"

"Hit man?" I said.

"If you think you need a gun to be a hit man, then think again," Bowlman said. "Not in this day and age. The writ, the suit, the threatening letter, have all the firepower they need. But this time"—he wagged his finger—"they picked the wrong guy."

"What are you going to do?" I said.

"Take them all the way to the Supreme Court," Bowlman said.

"But won't that be very expensive?" I said.

"Not if I represent myself, which is exactly what I plan to do. I have my speech all worked out: 'Ladies and gentlemen of the Supreme Court, today is your chance to strike a mighty blow for the little guy.' You should have seen the look on Borg's face when I told him. Surprise, buddy boy—the little guy bites back."

I thought of the list from the briefcase, with the Schlecks first and Rewind Enterprises second. Was it a list of little guys who bit back? "Do you know Tim and Maria Schleck?" I said.

"Nope," said Bowlman.

At that moment, the door opened and a man entered. He looked somewhat like Bowlman, although with a less luxuriant ponytail. "*Eddie Cochran, Live at Town Hall Party,* 1959?" he said. "You're my last hope."

"Give me a hard one," said Bowlman.

• • •

We all went home, Silas splitting off first, then Tut-Tut, leaving Ashanti and me together. As we turned onto our street, we saw a TV truck in front of Tim and Maria Schleck's burned-out place, now behind fire department barricades. They had bright lights set up, lights that shone on the faces of an interviewer holding a mic and the interviewee, a tall handsome man with swept-back silvery hair and a nice fresh-looking tan: Sheldon Gunn. We went closer.

". . . a terrible tragedy," Sheldon Gunn was saying, "losing such an irreplaceable old building."

"How long have you owned it, Mr. Gunn?" said the interviewer.

"Oh, not too long, a year or so, perhaps. But as Brooklynites know, I'm a great one for historic preservation, so naturally I'm just devastated by this. Thank God the tenants—such a lovely young couple—were unharmed."

"What are your plans for the site?" the interviewer said.

"Oh, too soon to say," said Gunn. "But you can be assured we'll do whatever is in the best interest of the neighborhood and the borough as a whole."

The interviewer leaned forward. I noticed that while her hair was soft and blond and fluffy, her face was hard and narrow. "How do you respond," she said, "to critics who say the New Brooklyn Redevelopment Project is just an instrument for driving the poor out of the borough?"

Gunn smiled, his teeth big and white and perfect. Sometimes, like when the eyes don't join in, a fake smile is easy to spot, but Gunn's eyes—small and grayish—were joining in. "Personally, Dina, I'm unaware of any such criticism. But if critics are out there, please come forward, identify yourselves, speak up. I guarantee you'll have our full attention."

"Thank you, Mr. Gunn," the interviewer said. "Dina DiNunzio, reporting from Brooklyn. Back to the studio."

Sheldon Gunn and Dina DiNunzio didn't speak another word to each other. The bright lights went out, and the crew packed up. The other spectators, maybe a dozen, moved on. Gunn buttoned up his topcoat and turned toward his limo, parked a few doors farther down, but as he turned, he saw us. Saw me, to be accurate, and paused.

"You don't think he's coming—" Ashanti began.

But he was. He walked toward us, raised his eyebrows—thin and snow-colored—and said, "Robbie?"

He remembered my name, just from that single meeting outside Bread? That was a shocker. The silver heart started fluttering against my wrist. I got the idea—completely crazy—that it was afraid.

"Um, hi, Mr. Gunn."

"Ah, you remember me," he said. "How is your lovely mother these days?"

"Uh, fine."

"And who's this bright-looking friend of yours?"

"Ashanti," I said. "Ashanti, this is Mr. Gunn."

He held out his hand. Very slowly, Ashanti extended hers. Their eyes met. Ashanti's were icy; Gunn's sparkled for a moment, like he was amused about something.

"Pleasure to meet you, Ashanti," he said. "And what a special name. A stroke of luck, running into your friend Robbie like this. You know why?"

Ashanti shook her head.

Gunn turned to me. "Because a very strange thing happened that morning we met outside that soup kitchen." He paused. "Any idea what it was?"

I shook my head.

"None?" he said.

"No."

"What if I gave you three guesses?"

I felt myself squirming inside. This grown-up, this billionaire, was toying with a couple of kids. An answer came to me out of nowhere, and I blurted it out. "You suddenly felt what it's like when the cupboard is bare?"

He went still. So did Ashanti. Gunn's face hardened in a way I'd never seen on anyone before, as though the skull beneath the skin was coming through. A long, long moment went by, and then he smiled, and in a flash, the illusion, if that was what it was, disappeared and he looked normal again, meaning normal for a rich, rested, handsome, and powerful middle-aged guy.

"No, no," he said. "Nothing so strange as that. But an interesting idea—I give you credit. I simply lost something that morning, but it might have been earlier or later. I didn't notice until the afternoon. Maybe I was the victim of a common pickpocket, not that I'm suggesting that criminal types necessarily congregate around soup kitchens."

"What did you lose?" Ashanti said, pushing this way too far, in my opinion.

Gunn gave Ashanti a close look, just for a second, but in the second, I got the idea that some machine inside him switched on and scanned her mind. He was very smart, no doubt about that. "Nothing that can't be replaced," Gunn said. "Many times over." He noticed his driver holding open the rear door of the limo. "Ah," he said, "mustn't keep Hector waiting." He took a last look at the burned-out building. "So fortunate no one was hurt," he said. Gunn got in the car, glanced out at us. "A pleasure running into you two. Take care." Hector closed the door.

20

When I got home, different-colored index cards were scattered all over the kitchen table. Index cards didn't appear often, always meant my dad was having trouble with his book. I read a green one: *Max gets an old memory wrong.* And a blue one: *someone else's dry cleaning gets delivered, which means???*

Dad came into the room, a mug of coffee in his hand.

"Hi, Dad. Who's Max?"

"That's the question, all right." He moved a few of the cards around with his fingertip. "It could almost be the title of the book."

Who's Max? Didn't do much for me. "Have you got a title yet?" I said. Titles were a total pain and very important at the same time, something I'd heard Dad and his writer friends talking about more than once.

"The working title is *Magic Spaces,*" he said. "Or

possibly *A Magic Space.* Or maybe *The Magic Space.* There's also . . ." He got a faraway look in his eyes, then shook his head.

"Wait," I said. "The book's about magic?"

"In a broad sense."

"Like, um?"

"Exalted states, I guess you'd say, their inevitable tendency to disappoint. The illusory triumph of the subjective and the relentlessness of the objective."

I didn't get any of that, but pressed on anyway. "What kind of powers do the characters have?"

"There's really only one character, in the traditional sense of story."

I nodded. I'd never read a story with only one character, but I knew, also from hearing my dad and his writer friends, that publishers were always on the lookout for new things, so maybe this was good. "Okay," I said, "this character—what are his powers?"

"Powers?"

"Magic powers," I said. "X-ray vision, for example."

My dad laughed, leaned forward, mussed up my hair a little. "The story may have experimental aspects, but it's still grounded in reality."

"I don't understand."

"Magic powers of the kind you're talking about don't exist, as I'm sure you're aware," Dad said. "They're just fantasy, child's play, or, at best, wishful thinking."

"Oh," I said.

My dad gave me a smile. "You're a great kid, you know that?"

"Thanks, Dad."

He checked his watch. "How does dinner in Manhattan sound? There's this new Indonesian place in Alphabet City, not even officially open yet, should be good."

"Okay."

He handed me some money. "I'm having a drink with Shep and his agent. Take a cab to Jane's office, and I'll meet the two of you at the restaurant."

I took a cab to my mom's office. The thing with cab drivers was you said the location you wanted and then added "that's near X," so they knew you weren't some tourist they could take on a long meander. After that, you could sit back, relax, and enjoy the view. I saw a seagull perched on a high girder of the Brooklyn Bridge, its wings folded in tight, maybe on account of the cold.

The taxi dropped me off in front of my mom's building in Lower Manhattan. I paid the driver, adding a tip. Dad said to tip fifteen percent, but that made the math hard, so I tipped twenty. I went inside to the security desk.

"Here to see Jane Forester at Jaggers and Tulkinghorn," I said, handing over my Thatcher ID, which sported the most horrible picture taken since the invention of photography. The guard turned the book so I could sign and printed a visitor's pass. I clipped it to my jacket, crossed the inner lobby, deserted on a Saturday afternoon, and entered an open elevator. Everything gleamed in my mom's building, including the insides of the elevators. I pressed seventy-eight and gazed at my reflection on the shiny walls. An idea hit me out of the blue: maybe I should try wearing my hair in a side part. I tried parting it on the right, the left, and the right again. The doors opened. Jaggers and Tulkinghorn had the whole seventy-eighth floor—and the seventy-ninth—so you were in the office the moment you left the elevator. No one was at the reception desk. I walked about half-way down a long hall to a closed door with my mom's name on it, and knocked.

"Come in," Mom called, in her office voice.

I went in.

"Hi, Mom."

She looked up from her work. "Hi, Robbie. I won't be long. Have fun with Ashanti?"

"Yeah."

"What did you do?"

"Hung out."

"Did you see Chas?"

"Yeah."

"What's he doing?"

"The index cards."

"Oh, my."

"Yeah."

Her gaze returned to the big stack of papers in front of her, almost like it was in the grip of some magnetic field. She frowned, scratched out a line or two, wrote in something else. "Some new magazines arrived," she said, not looking up.

"Okeydoke."

She looked up suddenly. "What have you done to your hair?"

"Just trying a side part." I didn't bother asking if she liked it, the answer already clear.

Mom's office wasn't huge, but it did have a little lounge-type setup in the corner—two-seater couch, comfy chair, coffee table—for having whatever kind of conversations with clients that you didn't have at the desk. I sat in the comfy chair and leafed through some magazines. The models, celebrities, and actresses all seemed to have cool parts in their hair.

"Sorry if you're bored," my mom said, some time later.

"I'm not bored." But I was, and Mom was good at sensing that kind of thing.

"There's a TV in the upstairs boardroom," she said. "It'll be empty. I'll come up when I'm done."

"Okay."

I took the elevator. Seventy-nine, where the partners had their offices, was fancier than seventy-eight, with Persian rugs scattered on the marble hallway and vases of flowers all over the place. The upstairs boardroom was at the end. It had a highly polished oval table made of some dark wood, with a couple of dozen leather chairs around it. A big flat screen hung on one wall. I found the remote and sat in one of the end chairs, maybe where the big boss partner—not Jaggers or Tulkinghorn, both long dead—sat when important decisions, like about the size of my mom's bonus, were being made.

"How's fifty mill sound?" I said. "No objections? Done!" And I was about to switch on the TV when I heard footsteps in the hall. I glanced down the table toward the open doorway, just in time to catch sight of a man going by. He was putting on a dark coat, switching his briefcase from one hand to another. But I hardly noticed those details. What grabbed my attention was the perfect profile, the silvery blue of the eye I could see, and the platinum hair. In other words: Egil Borg.

He kept going, without a look my way, and passed from view. But I fully expected him to wheel around the next second—how could anyone miss the sound of my pounding heart?

No wheeling around happened. I sat motionless in

the big boss partner chair. There was only one door to the upstairs boardroom, meaning only one way out. Time passed. I rose—every movement almost painfully careful—walked around the table, and halted just short of the doorway. Then I thought, *Whoa! Get a grip.* I had every right to be here, visitor's pass lawfully in place. I took a deep breath and stepped into the hall.

Deserted. I walked a normal type walk to the elevators. The indicator light showed them all at L, except for one still on its way down. Four, three, two, L. It stayed there; they all stayed there, safe at L. I headed back along the hall, past the boardroom, reading the names on every door until I came to E. Borg. Door closed, almost certainly locked. But just to be thorough, I gave the knob an exploratory twist. And it turned. So what else could I do but give the door an exploratory push? It opened. I entered the office of Egil Borg, troubleshooter and fixer for Jaggers and Tulkinghorn.

Egil Borg's office was smaller than my mom's and had no little sitting area. The window was bigger than hers, but the blinds were down, admitting thin bands of light through the slats. Also my mom's office had her college and law school diplomas on the walls, plus lots of pictures of me, my dad, and Pendleton, and some cool posters of Provence—her favorite place on earth and where we were going to spend a whole month at some future period when she could get the time off. Borg's walls were completely bare, except for a full-length mirror—I checked my side part again: really that bad?—and one small framed photo of an unsmiling old guy in a military helmet. I went closer and read his name—Patton—and was no wiser.

So mostly this office was about things not being there. The main thing in it was the huge desk, shaped like a rounded L and made of black metal. There was nothing on it except a phone, a big monitor, and a sleek little keyboard. The screen was blank. I touched the *x* key, just to see what would happen.

The screen lit up and a message appeared: *Password Please.* I had an amazing intuition: the password *was* please. So I typed it: *p-l-e-a-s-e.*

Things happened fast after that, so fast and confusing I really can't trust my memory to be accurate. But first a little square at the top of the monitor flashed. Camera! That little square was a camera, of course, and now it had just snapped my picture, capturing a record of what I was up to at that moment, which happened to be trespassing and breaking into someone's computer. Proof beyond a shadow of a doubt. A whole bad chain of future events unreeled in my mind, events that included my mom getting fired and my dad pounding the pavement in search of real—I meant other—work, and me in cuffs. Then came the power, instantaneous and free of pain, shock, or headache. The red-gold beam, brighter than I'd ever seen it, flared out and struck that little square at the top of the monitor. I heard a soft sizzling sound, saw a tiny puff of smoke. Meaning what? I didn't know.

I backed away from the computer, sidestepping out of its range, pocketing my glasses. My first thought, an especially stupid one, was to sneak up on the computer from behind, kick it off the desk, and jump up and down on it, leaving nothing but digital innards. But then what? Leave the innards on the floor? Somewhere in those busted-up innards, I was pretty sure, would lie my picture, waiting for some nerd to find it. That—*nerd*—led me to a useful thought: Silas.

Silas would know what to do. I was reaching for my phone, foreseeing all sorts of problems, like what if I couldn't reach him, or what if he couldn't tell me on the phone but had to come in person, when a problem I wasn't foreseeing suddenly presented itself.

Ding. A soft, quiet ding, a familiar sound I couldn't place for a second, and then did. It was the signal made by an elevator just coming to a stop. After that one ding: silence. Maybe this was one of those times when an elevator stops at a floor for no reason, opens and closes its door, and goes away. I listened my hardest, hoping for more silence. And yes! My hopes were answered. Silence and nothing but sweet, sweet—

But no. A footstep sounded—the hard-heeled footstep

of a businessman's shoe—and then more: *clack clack clack.* After that, no sound. Had whoever he was gone into his office, somewhere down the hall? *Clack clack clack.* No, he'd merely passed over one of those Persian rugs. Another brief silence and then again *clack clack clack,* closer and closer. I glanced around wildly, looking for a place to hide—like behind a two-seater couch, say, which this Spartan office didn't have. *Clack clack clack.* There was nowhere to hide but under the big desk shaped like a rounded L. I darted underneath, pushing the wastebasket aside.

And right away realized what a dumb hiding place it was: surprisingly well-lit and not very spacious, considering the size of the desk. Also—but there was no time to consider the alsos. *Clack clack clack.* From my angle down on the floor, I saw the shoes first. Businessman's shoes: these were called wingtips, I thought, on account of the toe cap part having perforations shaped like two wings spreading along the sides. Then the cuffs of the dark gray woolen pants, and the lower leg parts, sharply creased. The briefcase was set down on the floor, just inches from me, a fine briefcase stamped with two small gold letters: *EB.* The hand setting it down was big and strong. I smelled coffee and tuna. Egil Borg hadn't left for the day, but only nipped out for a snack.

He sat in his chair, stretched his legs. I squeezed back against the hard inner frame of the desk as far as I could, his shoe tips an inch away. Any moment now he was going to—yes, I heard him tapping at the keyboard.

He went still. He drew his legs back, leaned forward, said, "Hmmm." In the next second or two he'd be looking at the image of a girl who turned out to be a moron. More tapping and then: "What's this?"

What's this, meaning my goose was cooked? Or what's this, meaning he was puzzled about something? It sounded more like that second kind of what's this, but I couldn't be sure, and before anything happened to clear things up, his phone rang.

He swiveled in the chair and reached for the phone. I caught a glimpse of his strong jaw and downturned mouth.

"Borg," he said.

The voice on the other end sounded small and tinny, but I recognized the speaker: Sheldon Gunn. He asked a question, something about a secure phone.

"Of course," said Borg.

Gunn spoke again. I could pick out a few words, like *situation* and *time* and *essence*.

"Not sure I understand," Borg said.

Gunn's voice rose, and now I got every word. "Are you paid to understand?"

"Yes," said Borg. And then backing down a little: "Within limits."

Gunn was quiet for a few seconds. "That's true," he

said, "and is even part of what makes you useful. Useful within limits."

One of Borg's legs began doing a jittery little thing. He extended it suddenly, kicking me right on the kneecap, a hard spot that must have felt desklike to him. "Ow" came oh so close to popping out of my mouth, but it didn't, and then Gunn was talking, his voice low and hard to hear again. I picked out a few phrases, like "the Saudis are getting impatient" and "financing deadline" and "speed, speed, speed."

"Got that," said Borg, "but we'll have to change tactics."

Gunn's voice rose. "Why?"

"Otherwise we'll arouse suspicions."

"Didn't you take care of that blogger?"

Slight pause. "The blog is down."

"Then no one will connect the dots," Gunn said. "There have been pyromaniacs before, there will be pyromaniacs again."

"All right," said Borg, "but we'll need more cash."

Gunn, his voice low again, said something about short sales and hung up. Short sales were something about the stock market. My dad had tried it once, with bad results.

Silence. After a few moments, Borg burst out with a string of bad language, then punched a key on his phone.

"Henkel?" he said, his tone changed now, much more commanding. "New schedule. Twelve thirty tonight. The Goat." *Click.*

Twelve thirty tonight? The Goat? Something real bad was in the near future. My only chance now was to stay unnoticed until Borg left the office. *Leave, split, up and at 'em,* I thought, willing him my hardest to go. But he didn't go, instead leaned forward and tapped again at his keyboard.

"Something happened here," he muttered. He sniffed the air. "But what?"

Had he already seen my picture? What was going on?

More tapping. Then the sound of him sipping his coffee. "Yech," he said, and compared the taste of the coffee to dog pee, although pee was not the word he used. Then he lowered the coffee cup—a paper cup with KWIK KOFFEE written on the side—down into my field of vision. He moved it first in one direction, then another, like he was searching for something like—oh, no!—the wastebasket. But the wastebasket wasn't in its usual place, on account of me having moved it.

I got hold of the wastebasket—gently, gently—and began to slide it toward a spot underneath that coffee cup. Suddenly Borg made a sweeping movement and his hand brushed against mine and then bumped the rim of the wastebasket. He dropped the coffee cup inside. His hand lingered there for a moment, feeling the wastebasket rim, then patting at the air around it. I shrank back, just out of reach, not even breathing. I could smell his breath: coffee, tuna, breath mint. He patted the air some more, his strong fingers—tiny tufts of platinum hair grew between the knuckles—coming an inch from my nose. His hand paused there, and then after what seemed like centuries, moved to the wastebasket. He adjusted its position back to exactly where it had been originally, straightened in his seat, and turned to the computer.

Tap-tap-tap.

21

Egil Borg, fixer and troubleshooter, worked away on his computer. I stayed where I was, motionless under his desk, smelling coffee and tuna, and sensing his bad mood pressing against me like a material thing.

"Blank?" he said after a while. "How can it be blank? What's been going on here?" He kicked out again with one of his feet, nailing my knee once more, exact same spot, with his fancy wingtip. This time it hurt even worse than before.

I rubbed my knee. This—staying under the desk and getting kicked from time to time—couldn't go on. I was starting to get the picture, which was all about the lack of a picture, specifically mine. That was what was annoying Borg so much. He must have been thinking that his camera, or his programming, or some other thing that Silas would understand had screwed up. So soon he'd be giving up, right? Calling it a day and going home. I was starting to get a cramp in my leg, but there was no way to straighten it without bumping into one of those wingtips.

Meanwhile Borg was back to tapping at the keys. A fixer and troubleshooter, yes, but also a lawyer, and I knew lawyers could stay at their desks for long, long sessions. Was it possible to somehow crawl out from under the desk, across the room, and out the door? I moved ever so slightly, not even crawling, more like the wriggling of a very slow worm, just enough to peek out from behind the corner of the desk and check the position of the door: a football field away, and closed.

At that very moment, someone knocked on it.

"Who is it?" said Borg, sounding impatient and unfriendly.

"I.T.," said a man on the other side of the door.

"Come in."

A man in jeans and a T-shirt came in, carrying a tool kit.

"What took you so long?" Borg said.

"Uh, sorry," said the I.T. guy. "What can I do you for?"

"I hate that expression," Borg said. The I.T. guy's mouth opened, but he didn't say anything. "Someone entered a wrong password," Borg told him. "The camera is programmed to take a picture of anyone doing that, but I can't find it. I need that photo, and I need it pronto."

"I'll see what I can do," said the I.T. guy.

"Just do it," Borg told him.

"Yes, sir."

The I.T. man approached the desk. I ducked out of sight. He came around the back. I was just noticing that he wore big heavy boots when one of them came right down on the back of my hand.

It hurt! And the cramp in my leg was hurting, too. Those twin hurts teamed up to try and make me utter some cry, but I kept it inside.

The I.T. guy, one booted foot still on my hand, put his tool kit on the desk, leaned forward, and got to work.

"Well, well," he said after a while.

"What's that supposed to mean?" said Borg.

"Fried," said the I.T. guy.

"What are you talking about?"

"Lens, circuitry, the whole photo library," the I.T. guy said. "All wiped out."

"You're saying you can't retrieve the photo?"

"No way."

"How could that happen?" Borg said.

"Must've been a power surge," said the I.T. guy, not sounding very sure.

"Haven't we got surge protection?"

"Best there is, but there's no guarantee that—"

"And if there was a power surge how come the rest of the computer's fine?"

"That's a head-scratcher, actually," said the I.T. guy. "Kind of unprecedented, in my experience. I could take it down to the shop, maybe run a couple of—"

"You're dismissed," Borg said.

The I.T. guy packed up, stepped off my hand, and left the room. The pattern of his boot heel lingered on my skin. I was gazing at it and flexing my hand a bit, when I realized I was still seeing very clearly without my glasses; the power was in no hurry to leave me.

"What a moron," Borg said; I'm leaving out an adjective he put before moron. He smacked the desk, then rose and started pacing around, out of my line of sight. "Memo to self," he said. "Have I.T. moron fired." He paused. I could feel him thinking. Then he was on the move again. I heard the door open, heard him walking onto the hard floor of the hall; the door slammed shut.

I made myself count to sixty. But why? I thought, when I got to fifty-nine. What if Borg had just been in need of more pacing territory and was on his way back? I squeezed out from under the desk, rose, straightened out my cramped leg with both hands, and limped across Borg's office.

Very slow, very careful, I turned the knob, opened

the door an inch or two, and peered out. No one in the hall. I hurried to the elevator bank. One elevator stood open. I jumped inside, hit seventy-eight. The doors closed. The elevator started moving. I took a deep breath, one of those sighs of relief, and at that moment saw myself in the shiny elevator walls. Hey! I looked kind of the way I did in Tut-Tut's drawing. And one other thing: my side part was gone. I felt around on my head: no part. Had I taken the part out sometime after leaving my mom's office and going up to seventy-nine? No. And therefore? The power didn't like the part either? I searched for some other explanation.

I went into my mom's office.

"All set?" she said. "I was just coming up to get you."

"All set," I said.

"Where are your glasses?"

"In my pocket."

"Well, put them on—you don't want to strain your eyes."

I put on my glasses, straining my eyes. The power wanted to stay a little longer.

"Mom?" I said. We were in a taxi, on the way to meet my dad at the Indonesian place. "What's financing?"

She glanced at me. "Financing is about providing funds for business or investing."

"Funds means money?"

"Basically."

"What do the Saudis have to do with it?"

"The Saudis?"

"I heard the Saudis do financing."

"Who told you that?"

"I just heard people talking about it."

"Well," said my mom, "the Saudis—meaning the royal family and the ruling class—have lots and lots of money from all these years of selling their oil. You can't just let money sit there—"

"Why not?"

"Because almost always it will be worth less the next day."

Not sure I got that—in fact, I knew I hadn't—but Mom was already going on.

"So you have to put the money to work—backing some tech start-up, for example, or buying up an already existing company, or lending to a developer."

"Like a real estate developer?"

"Exactly."

"The poor kind of real estate developer," I said.

"The poor kind?" said Mom.

"Because the rich kind—like Sheldon Gunn—wouldn't need financing. He'd use his own money."

My mom smiled. "Sheldon Gunn seems to have made quite an impression on you."

I shrugged. "Just using him as an example," I said. "Could be any big developer."

"Such as?" Mom said.

I tried to think of a name, got nowhere.

My mom laughed. "Even the Sheldon Gunns of the world need financing. Being a billionaire doesn't mean you have quick access to the huge amounts of cash that the New Brooklyn Redevelopment Project will need. Just using that as an example." Mom has this look my dad calls her checkmate face. She gave it to me now.

I laughed. So did she. We sat a little closer together in the back of the taxi.

"And using other people's money often makes sense for a lot of reasons," Mom said, "such as tax avoidance or estate pla— Driver! You missed the turn."

Back home after dinner at the Indonesian restaurant— my vision returning to its terrible normal self with the arrival of the menus—texts zoomed around between Ashanti, Silas, and me, but not Tut-Tut since he had no cell phone. I kept the whole Borg adventure out of it, stuck to the fact that something was going down at the Red Goat that night at twelve thirty and we just had to be there. But how? We were kids, and it was night. I couldn't just say, "Hey, I'm going out for a stroll, be back whenever."

Downstairs, I could hear Mom and Dad talking about

Shep and the agent. The drinks thing had gone well—the agent liked having a title with *Magic* in it, and he'd asked to see the first fifty pages, so Dad had his work cut out for him, since there weren't any pages yet. Dad said something, and Mom laughed. It was nice to hear them having fun like that, but weren't they tired? Wasn't it sleepy time? I went to my window and gazed down at our garden—a small space with a brick patio and a dirt patch where Mitch tried to grow tomatoes. On the far side stood a building much like ours, and on each side grew cherry trees that never produced cherries. Past the cherry tree on the left was a narrow alley that led to the street on the block behind us. Right outside my window was the fire escape. I've climbed out there once or twice in summer to catch a few rays—my little secret.

I raised the window. Cold air blew into my room. I stepped out onto the fire escape. It was like a narrow, railed-in balcony with a square hole in the middle of the floor. You stepped through that hole to the ladder that slanted down to a similar balcony on the next floor, which happened to be outside the downstairs bathroom window. That balcony didn't have a hole; instead you walked to the end and lowered the ladder, left in the up position to keep the burglars at bay. My parents had explained the whole setup when we'd moved in. I'd never tried it, of course. It was all theory.

I climbed back inside and closed the window. There was a knock at the door.

"Yeah?" I said.

"I feel a draft," my mom said. Mom was a champion feeler of drafts. The door opened and she popped her head in. "No wonder," she said. "It's so cold in here." She glanced at the window, saw it was closed, and felt the radiator. "Nice and warm," she said, looking puzzled. She was moving toward the window when Dad looked in.

"What's going on?" he said.

"Mom feels a draft."

Dad laughed, said, "What's new?" and moved off down the hall to their bedroom. Mom smiled and shook her head in a what-can-I-do way. They were both in a pretty good mood; we'd have to hit that Indonesian place more often.

"Night, Robbie. Don't stay up too late."

"Night, Mom."

She closed the door and left. Soon there were running-water sounds and moving-around sounds and then things got quiet.

I called Ashanti, spoke very low. "I can get out," I said.

"Me too," said Ashanti, "but only after my mother takes her sleeping pill."

"When will that be?"

"I don't know. She's pretty lively tonight."

"What's she doing?"

"Listening to music."

"Oh."

"Opera," Ashanti says. "She loves opera, especially Maria Callas."

"Who's that?"

"This singer," Ashanti said. "Unbearable."

"What about Silas?" I said.

"He says he might be able to get out of his apartment, but he can't figure how to handle the doorman."

"With a tip, right?"

Ashanti laughed.

"Tell you what," I said, some part of my mind pretty much making the decision on its own, without involvement from me. "I'm going to the Red Goat. Meet me there if you can make it."

"I'll make it."

22

Not long after by the clock—but it sure seemed long—our apartment was silent, except for the odd moan from Pendleton, having a nightmare under my desk, his normal sleeping spot, even though he had a comfy dog bed in the front hall. Eleven thirty: time to go. I walked softly across my room, opened my closet, and picked out the kind of outfit that seemed right for whatever was about to happen: jeans, my last-year's jacket (navy blue, instead of the new one, with its white shoulder patches), my black sneakers. I pocketed all the money I happened to have in my room—$5.50. Then I took a deep breath, opened my window, and stepped onto the fire escape. Decision one: Close the window completely, meaning there was no guarantee I could reopen it? Leave it wide open? Leave it open a crack? I left it open a crack. That risked a tiny draft, yes, but my bedroom door and my mom's door were both closed, and besides she and Dad slept under a thick down comforter that had to be practically draftproof.

Step one: down the fire escape. As I moved toward the square space where the ladder began, something cold and damp touched my face. I glanced up and saw a few snowflakes falling from the dark pink nighttime sky. I turned around, stepped on the second rung from the top and started down, my sneakers making tiny squeaks on the cold steel.

At the next level, outside our downstairs bathroom window, I examined the ladder that would take me to the ground. Nothing held it down: all I had to do was slide it forward, hook the two end thingies over the last railing on the platform, and—

Shatter! Uh-oh. The feet of the ladder struck something made of glass that must have been lying in the yard. It sounded like a plate glass window exploding. I went still, listening my hardest. Guitar music came from not far away, but there was only silence behind the wall of our building. No one had heard the noise, or it had been swallowed up in the sounds of the city.

She who hesitates is lost: that was what Ms. Kleinberg always said when she was trying to get us to take the open shot. I climbed down the ladder, walked quickly into the alley, and headed for the street.

Snowflakes drifted through the air in ones and twos. The cars and buses going by had their wipers on, but there wasn't much traffic, and hardly any walkers at all. No one took any notice of me. I picked up the pace. After not too long I was passing Joe Louis, the school yard deserted at this hour, of course—except that it wasn't. Over in the far corner sat a small figure, back against the chain-link fence.

The gate to the yard was locked, but there was a hole in the fence big enough for someone my size to walk through without even stooping. I walked through, crossed the yard, reached the small figure sitting in the corner, snowflakes landing on his dreads.

"Tut-Tut?" I said. "What are you doing here?"

He looked up. Even in those low-light conditions, I could see that something was wrong. Tut-Tut's upper lip was swollen on the left side, and there was a cut above his left eye. One of the characters in *On/Off* dreamed of being a boxer, although he was actually a dental office supply salesman, so my dad read tons about boxing for a month or so, and one thing I learned was that right-hand punches land on the left side of the other guy's face.

"Oh, no," I said. "Your uncle?"

He nodded, just a little nod, hardly any movement at all.

"Why didn't you go to HQ?"

He shrugged. That shrug was one of the saddest things I'd ever seen.

"Come on," I said, extending my hand. "It's starting

to snow." His eyes shifted. He tracked a falling snowflake and the expression on his face began to change,
leaving pure misery behind. Tut-Tut took my hand. I
helped him up. A cold gust of wind rippled the thin fabric of his hoodie. That was all he wore—the hoodie, plus
tattered jeans and my old sneakers, one of the laces now
missing. "How about wearing my gloves for a bit?" I
said.

He thrust his hands quickly into the warmer on the
hoodie and shook his head. No way I could abandon
Tut-Tut out in the cold. Somehow he had to come home
with me. Was there time? I checked on my phone: 11:57.
No. So therefore?

"There's some news," I said. "On the robbing-from-
the-rich front."

Tut-Tut looked interested.

"I'll have to tell you on the way."

We walked fast, snow starting to fall a little more heavily
now, but melting the moment it hit pavement. I told Tut-
Tut about Borg's conversations with Sheldon Gunn and
the long-nosed guy, even mentioned the part about the
Saudis, none too clear in my own mind. I watched Tut-
Tut carefully as I told him. He didn't even break stride,
simply nodded, like if I was saying it, then it had to make
sense.

We came to the bridge over the canal. On the far side stood the Red Goat. Still lopsided, but lights shone inside, customers were at the bar, and Big Nanny was back in her place over the door. Hey! That was our doing!

Tut-Tut and I crossed the bridge. Down below, the canal looked sluggish and green, like it was made of some oily gel; falling snowflakes turned black on the surface and vanished at once. I checked the time: 12:24. Something was about to happen, but what? I walked right up to the window of the Red Goat and peered inside. There were maybe seven or eight people inside, but the only one I recognized was Duke behind the bar, an overhead light gleaming on his shaved head.

Tut-Tut spoke behind me. "B-b-b-b—"

I turned. Tut-Tut had crossed the street and was gazing at the canal. I ran over. Something was moving out there. A boat? Yes, a boat, which was Tut-Tut had been trying to tell me. The boat had no lights showing, except for the display panel at the console, its dull greenish light reflecting on the face of the driver: Egil Borg. As the boat came closer, Tut-Tut and I shrank back against a huge and rotting bollard that rose up from the depths of the canal. My uncle Joe had a powerboat a lot like this one, maybe not quite as long, but with the same sort of big cabin in the bow. He'd taken me waterskiing behind it the summer before, if getting up for the odd second or two counted as waterskiing. But Uncle Joe's engine was much noisier; Borg's made a low purr. Borg glided his boat to a stop at the foot of the bridge, tied up to a post, climbed onto dry land, and started up the stone stairs that led to the street. A closed and locked gate stood at the top of the stairs—you weren't supposed to go down there—but it wasn't high, and Borg vaulted over in one easy motion.

Tut-Tut and I slid around the bollard, staying in its shadow. Borg didn't cross the street, but moved a few steps closer to us, where a second bollard stood, and stayed there; in the shadows, just like us. He waited. So did we.

The snow started coming harder. I'm a big lover of snow, but at the moment, I was way too nervous to enjoy it. Tut-Tut, on the other hand, had his damaged face turned up to the sky, and wonder in his eyes. He stuck out his tongue and caught a snowflake.

A taxi came down the street, stopping by the Red Goat. The back door opened, and out stepped the long-nosed guy, the guy with the briefcase who'd gone all ecstatic at the sight of the Schlecks' fire. And now I had a name for him: Henkel. And his occupation, straight from Sheldon Gunn: pyromaniac.

Henkel closed the door, and the taxi drove off. He glanced around. Borg made a little *psst-psst* sound. Hen-

kel crossed the street and joined him. They moved behind the bollard. Tut-Tut and I moved, too, just enough
to see them without being seen, we hoped.

"You're late," Borg said.

"Frickin' weather," said Henkel; he had a high, whiny
voice. "You try getting a cab."

There was a pause. Borg's voice, hard to begin with,
hardened some more. "Are you in or out?"

"Whoa," said Henkel. "In, for sure. Thought you
knew that."

"Then don't be late and don't make excuses," Borg
said.

"Okay, sorry."

"You remember what *out* means, Henkel?"

Henkel's voice got squeaky. "I said I was sorry."

"Do you know the most important difference between people?" Borg said.

"Some have money and some don't?"

Borg shook his head. "Some—that is to say most—
are replaceable. Others—the very few—are not."

"Huh," said Henkel. "I never knew that."

At that moment, a customer came out of the Red
Goat, throwing a shaft of light across the street. It illuminated Borg's eyes, and Henkel got a good look at the
expression in them.

"But now I do," he said quickly. "Much obliged."

The door of the Red Goat closed, cutting off the light. The customer walked off, talking to himself. "Snow," he said. "That's all I need."

Borg unzipped his jacket a few inches, reached in and took out a thick manila envelope. He handed it to Henkel.

"Hey, thanks," Henkel said.

But Borg hadn't let go. "No screwups," he said.

"Don't worry," said Henkel.

Borg laughed, a strange laugh, sharp and brief, that didn't sound amused in any way. "I'm a worrier, Henkel," he said. "Remember that." He let go of the envelope. Henkel tucked it away.

"No complaints last time, right?" he said, sounding more assertive, as though whatever was in the envelope had made him stronger. "I know my job."

"Aren't you going to count it?" Borg said.

"I trust you," said Henkel.

"That's wise of you," Borg said. "As for jobs, you're only as good as the next one. I'll be waiting down below for your report." He moved toward the gate, then paused. "And keep your eyes peeled."

"For what?" said Henkel.

"Any sort of trouble."

"Like?"

Borg glanced quickly around. Tut-Tut and I tried to

vanish into the bollard. "I don't know," Borg said. "I just sense something."

"The weather, most likely," said Henkel.

Borg gave him a look, not friendly, then vaulted back over the gate and disappeared down the stone stairs. Henkel turned and started toward the bridge.

23

e waited, Tut-Tut and I, until Henkel was halfway across the bridge. Then, without any signal between us, we both left the shadows of the bollard and started following. The wind had risen, and the snowflakes, so soft before, now carried a sting. A van went fishtailing by, and a man stood in front of a bodega scattering salt crystals from a bag, but hardly anyone else was around. Henkel walked quickly for a few blocks, never looking back, then stopped suddenly in a dark doorway. Dark, but not so dark that I missed the flash of the manila envelope. He was counting the money after all.

I glanced at Tut-Tut: he looked amused. Meanwhile Henkel was on the move again. He took a right at the next corner, hurried along for two more blocks, the sidewalk coated with enough snow now to capture his footprints; Henkel had huge feet, the turned-out kind. Then came a left, a few more blocks, and there we were, approaching Rewind.

Tut-Tut and I crossed the street, not making a sound, and crept on, shielded by parked cars. There were parked cars on the other side, too, including a small, boxy four-door right in front of Rewind. Henkel stopped behind it and glanced quickly around, Tut-Tut and I ducking out of sight. When we dared look again, peering through a small gap between two bumpers, we saw that Henkel had opened the trunk of the boxy car. He glanced around once more and lifted out something square and heavy. A container of some sort, kind of like . . . like the gasoline can my uncle Joe kept in his garage in the burbs, for fueling all his lawn-care machines.

Henkel closed the trunk real softly and turned toward Rewind; no lights showed inside. He set down the gas can, fumbled in his pocket for something, and huddled over the keyhole in the door. Faint scrape, scrape of metal on metal, and then the door was open. Henkel picked up the gas can and went inside, closing the door behind him.

And now? Tut-Tut and I rose and looked at each other. This would be a good moment for the power to put in an appearance, and . . . do something, I couldn't think exactly what. The silver heart dangled motionless from the bracelet.

"Feel anything?" I said.

Tut-Tut shook his head.

Rewind's windows were dark, and no sound came from within. "What are we going to do?" I said.

"S-s-s-s-suh-suh-suh—"

"Something?"

"Y-y-y-ye-," he said.

Tut-Tut and I crossed the street and went up to the door of Rewind. I grasped the knob and turned it, at the same time having a shameful wish: maybe the door wouldn't open and that would be that. But it did, nice and easy.

I pushed the door open, real slow. What if it was one of those doors that made a bell tinkle inside the shop? Had that happened when we'd entered before? I couldn't remember.

No bell tinkled. Tut-Tut and I stepped inside. He closed the door, very softly. A little light penetrated from the street, but petered out at about the halfway mark in the long, narrow space. We peered into the gloom. There were lots of shadows, none in motion. I heard a furnace start up somewhere below; other than that, silence. We moved toward the back of the store.

My eyes began to adjust to the darkness. I could make out the rows of record bins, and the square silhouettes of the hanging album covers. We reached the end of the bins and came to Bowlman's tiny office—just a desk and a single file cabinet, slightly illuminated by the pulsing sleeper light of a computer. Behind the desk stood the rear wall of the store. No sign of Henkel. I turned to Tut-Tut. He stood by the right-hand wall, seemed to be examining some concert posters pinned to it. I went closer, saw that the posters concealed a low, narrow, knobless door. Tut-Tut gave it a push, and it swung open.

We gazed at a rough wooden staircase leading to the basement. Light shone down there, weak and yellow. *Power, where are you?* I was considering a pause, just to give the power a chance, supposing it was unavoidably detained somewhere else, but Tut-Tut started down the stairs, and I went with him. I didn't know what was going through Tut-Tut's mind, but mine was busy trying to convince me that the power would come if needed.

There were lots of smells in the basement under Rewind, damp, musty, moldy; water dripped somewhere nearby. We came to the bottom of the stairs and found ourselves in a narrow sort of corridor, flanked on both sides by record albums stacked higher than our heads. Beyond the record albums, I could see lots of clutter: a rusty tricycle, bundled-up newspapers, a stained mattress. A bare bulb, source of the weak yellow light, hung from the ceiling. And one more thing: I smelled gasoline.

We reached the last stack of records and peered

around the corner. More clutter, more junk, cobwebs all over the place, and by the far wall, in the space between the furnace and the hot water tank: Henkel. He was bent over and shuffling backward, pouring a thin stream of gasoline from the can as he went. The sound of gasoline splashing on the cement floor seemed very loud, like waves crashing on a beach, but of course that was impossible.

Henkel started circling around the furnace, pouring gasoline. He could have looked up at any moment and seen us, but he was concentrating too hard for that, an intense expression on his face like he was an artist on a big project. He shook the last drops from the can, then backed toward us, stopping just a few feet away, almost within touching distance. Henkel was breathing hard, although the actual effort of pouring gasoline couldn't have been that great. He reached into his pocket and took out a cigarette lighter.

The power! It had to be now. One more second would be too late. But the power refused to come.

Henkel opened the lighter with a flick of his wrist. Then he pressed the igniting button with his thumb and a tall flame shot up. He drew back his arm to toss the lighter into the gasoline puddle by the furnace. And at that moment, Tut-Tut stepped forward and grabbed the lighter right out of Henkel's hand.

If I'd been Henkel, I'd have cried out in complete terror, but Henkel wasn't like me. He didn't make a sound, just whipped around real fast. Yes, there was fear in his eyes, but it faded as he saw what he was facing, meaning me and Tut-Tut.

There was a long pause. Then Henkel said, "You're a little young for playing with lighters, kid." He extended his hand toward Tut-Tut. "Better give it to me for safe keeping."

Tut-Tut snapped the lighter shut and put it in his pocket. We backed away.

Henkel's lips turned up in the fakest smile I'd ever seen. "Don't be afraid, kids," he said. "Nothing bad's going to happen. You're free to go, soon's I get my property back."

"Nothing bad's going to happen?" I said. "Like what you did to the Schlecks?" Which maybe wasn't smart, but even though I was scared, I was also angry, and that anger came bursting out.

Henkel's long nose was his most noticeable feature. His eyes, small and muddy-colored, came way down the list. But now an expression entered them that caught my attention big-time, an expression that was sick and nasty.

"Ah," he said. "Happen to know anything about a certain missing briefcase?" We said nothing. Henkel smiled. "What's that word? *Improvise?* Yeah, that's it.

Looks like we're going to have to improvise, starting with the happy fact of whose fingerprints are now on the lighter."

At that moment—why so late?—I saw that Henkel wore surgical gloves. The prints on the lighter? Those would be Tut-Tut's. And who was interested in fingerprints? Crime scene investigators. Was Henkel about to frame us for burning down Rewind? Wouldn't that mean—

Henkel reached into his pocket and pulled out a gun. I'd never seen a gun before, not a real one, except in the holsters of NYPD cops. This gun was short and stubby, with a black grip and a dull silver barrel. Henkel didn't point it anywhere in particular.

"What you two can do for me now," he said, "is move over thataway." He flicked the gun barrel in the direction of the gasoline circle he'd poured, the liquid now puddling here and there on the uneven floor.

Once my dad gave me a talk on avoiding abductions. *Don't get in the car. Resist from the start. Scream your head off.*

"I said move."

I thought about screaming my head off, but had a feeling that a scream right now might make the gun go off. On the other hand, I wasn't going anywhere near the gasoline. Tut-Tut and I didn't budge. We stood side by side, shoulders touching.

The sick, nasty look in Henkel's eyes grew sicker and nastier, all shiny and bright. "Want me to improvise some more?" he said. "Have it your way."

The barrel of the gun swung in a little arc and then went still, aimed right at Tut-Tut's heart.

"D-d-d-d-d-," said Tut-Tut.

"Cat got your tongue?" Henkel said.

"Stop!" I said. "Stop right now! You can't do this!"

"Yeah," said Henkel, not looking at me, but at Tut-Tut's chest, "I can. That's the deal. Don't be upset. They say where you two are going is a better place."

The knuckle of Henkel's trigger-finger whitened, like he was starting to apply pressure. I thought of trying to knock the gun from his hand, but he was too far away, and—

And then I thought, No buts. What was the point of buts? Henkel was about to shoot Tut-Tut in the heart. The next thing I knew I was in midair.

From the corner of his eye Henkel saw me coming, started turning, started swinging the gun in my direction. But not quite fast enough. I crashed into him at knee level. The gun went off, making an enormous roar in the confined space. Henkel lost his balance and staggered backward; but might not have fallen, except that he stepped into a pool of gasoline and his feet slipped out from under him. They shot straight up into the air—the gun flying free—and for a crazy instant Henkel seemed to hang upside down. Then he fell headfirst, landing on the hard floor with a sharp crack.

Henkel lay still, his eyes half open, the nasty, sick look no longer in them. Tut-Tut stepped forward and picked up the gun.

We knelt over Henkel. Tut-Tut put his ear real close to the end of Henkel's long nose.

"Is he dead?" I said. There was a horrible feeling in the pit of my stomach. I'd never seen a dead person before.

"N-n-n-n-," said Tut-Tut. And of course Tut-Tut had seen dead people, including his own parents. He took my hand, held it to the side of Henkel's neck. Henkel's pulse seemed strong and steady. A corner of the manila envelope protruded from under his jacket. Tut-Tut pulled it out and handed it to me. I opened it: a wad of cash, still inside.

We gazed down at Henkel: a terrible man, pyromaniac and professional arsonist, who'd been about to murder us and enjoy doing it—I'd never forget that sick, excited look in his eyes. Tut-Tut rose and walked away. I wasn't paying much attention, on account of feeling a little sick myself. When Tut-Tut returned, he had a roll of duct tape in his hands. I took a quick glance at his swollen lip and that cut over his eye: Tut-Tut's life, so much harder than mine, had left him better prepared for some things.

We wrapped up Henkel's arms and legs with duct tape, nice and tight like they do it on TV crime shows. Right as we finished, Henkel's cell phone rang from inside one of his pockets. Tut-Tut and I both jumped a mile. It rang and rang and went silent.

We climbed the stairs and laid Henkel's arson money on Bowlman's desk. I wrote *Rent* on the manila envelope in case Bowlman got confused. Then I picked up the phone and called 9-1-1. "There's an arsonist at Rewind in Brooklyn," I said. "Better come quick." The woman on the other end started in with a question. I hung up. We went outside, closing the door carefully behind us.

The world had turned white in our absence. Once in history class, Mr. Stinecki, way off topic and going on about some poem he'd read in *The New Yorker,* said that white was the color of death. All of a sudden I wanted to puke. I tried the burping method and felt better.

Tut-Tut was gazing at the snow, looking very happy about it. "Sn-sn-sn—"

Sirens started up, not too far away. We began walking, in no particular direction at first.

"Borg wanted Henkel to go back to the boat," I said after a block or two. "He's up to something."

Tut-Tut nodded.

"I wonder what."

He nodded again.

The wind was rising; the snow no longer fell straight, but at an angle that got sharper and sharper as we walked. I should have felt cold, instead felt too warm, if anything.

"Are you cold?" I said.

Tut-Tut shook his head.

The bridge appeared in the distance, lit by a streetlamp at the far end. A man was on it, coming our way, his elongated shadow gliding ahead of him. I knew that stride by now, quick and athletic: Borg. I grabbed Tut-Tut's arm. We ducked down a short flight of stairs that led to someone's basement apartment and crouched in the little protected place, out of the weather. A minute or two later, Borg hurried by, his boots just about at our eye level, crunching in the snow. He was looking straight ahead, his expression hard, angry, and maybe a little anxious as well.

We stayed where we were until he was out of sight.

"He's gone to check on Henkel?" I said.

"Y-y-ye-ye-," said Tut-Tut.

There'd be confusion at Rewind, with cops and firemen and Henkel in duct tape and probably Bowlman appearing on the scene. That gave us time. Without another word, we both started running, up to street level and toward the canal, slip-sliding in the snow. Tut-Tut laughed a little laugh; no snow in Haiti, I thought. We crossed the bridge, turned down the dark street—no lights showing now in the Red Goat—and paused before the gate that led down to Borg's boat. Borg had vaulted it easily. We climbed it, not so easily, and followed the stone stairs to the canal.

Borg's boat bobbed on the water, choppy water now, ruffled up by the weather. No lights showed aboard. We stood listening for a few moments; I heard nothing but the wind. I moved toward the stern, just to see the name of the boat. There was enough nighttime city light to read it: *Short Sail.* Whoa. *Short Sail?* Hadn't that come up recently? My mind went searching back: Borg's office, Borg needing more money, Gunn saying something about what I had taken to be short sales, meaning a stock market play for getting the cash. But Gunn had been talking about *Short Sail,* the name of the boat being some kind of rich-guy pun.

Fenders protected *Short Sail*'s hull, kept it about two feet from the concrete side of the canal. Without another thought, I stepped across that ribbon of water to the deck.

"Wh-wh-wh-wha-," Tut-Tut said.

"What are we doing?" I said. "What we do—robbing from the rich, giving to the poor. I think there's money on board."

Tut-Tut hesitated. At first I thought he doubted me.

Then I remembered that last sketch he'd drawn in our warehouse HQ, empty ocean and a small figure clinging to a wrecked mast.

"It's okay," I said.

Tut-Tut stepped across, and as he did, I realized it wasn't okay. We'd made a huge mistake: our footprints in the snow.

"Oh, my God," I said. "When he comes back, he'll know someone's been on board."

Tut-Tut understood at once. He whipped around to check our footprints on the stone stairs and beside the boat. And at that very moment, a huge gust of wind blew by. It swept over the footprints, leaving a surface as smooth and unbroken as cake icing.

"That was lucky," I said.

The silver heart seemed to flutter on my wrist, but that too might have been the wind.

We searched the boat, starting in the stern. Nothing there but lockers full of coiled rope, fishing rods and reels, lifejackets, an anchor. In the storage space under the center console, we found charts, sunblock, a tool kit. That left the forward cabin. We opened the narrow door and went inside.

It was bigger than the cabin on Uncle Joe's boat. First came a galley with a sink, small fridge, and stove on one side and a table on the other. After that, through another door, lay the sleeping berths, two on each side. No sign of money out in the open. I was kneeling to check under the nearest berth when I thought I heard something. I froze, and heard it again. A footstep on the deck, beyond doubt. Tut-Tut and I looked at each other. His eyes were wide. We glanced around, saw portholes, closed and way too small in any case. There was only one way out, back through the forward cabin and onto the deck.

Sounds came from the deck: someone moving around, the thud of ropes, and then an inboard engine starting up; it throbbed through the deck. Seconds later we were under way. Another negative: There was no money on board, not that we could find. And a third: Ashanti and Silas hadn't made it. Not a surprise—we were all kids, and it was very late.

hort Sail glided slowly along the canal, the engine purring softly but with a kind of contained power. Through the little portholes, I caught glimpses of storage tanks, loading docks, rusted-out equipment I didn't know the names for, all the sharp angles getting rounded by the snow. A seagull stood on a piling right at eye level and just feet away, back to the wind and wings folded over its chest. Tut-Tut was doing the same thing with his arms, like he was holding on to himself. I tried to look reassuring; didn't dare utter a word, of course: I could hear a voice crackling over a radio, and then, right outside the cabin, Borg said, "Roger."

Roger? People said Roger in real life? It meant they were in agreement, right? So what was Borg agreeing to? And where were we going? I didn't think the canal was very long, nothing like the Erie Canal, for example, but its actual route was unclear in my mind. Did it go as far as—

All of a sudden, the engine roared and we surged forward, the bow rising up out of the water. Tut-Tut and I went flying. I hit the cabin door hard; whatever Tut-Tut hit made a lot of noise. We landed together on the floor.

The engine got throttled back abruptly and Borg said, "What was that?"

I motioned to Tut-Tut real quick. He rolled under one of the berths, and I scrambled under the next one, squeezed in next to a big duffel bag. The door burst open in a second. Borg, visible to me from the knees down, meaning mostly his thick black boots, came inside. He walked to the far end, returned. I heard him open some kind of compartment and slam it shut. He opened another one, moved some things around inside it. Then came a click as he closed it up. He paused. Was he thinking about rearranging more stuff, like maybe under the berths?

Power? Are you there?

No sign of the power, but Borg turned, both boots now pointed toward the stern. He walked out of the cabin and shut the door. A few seconds later, the engine roared and *Short Sail* surged forward again. I slid along the deck under the berth until I hit something fairly soft, possibly another duffel bag, making a thud that I hoped was dull. I glanced sideways and saw Tut-Tut clinging with both hands to the post that supported one corner of his berth. We stayed just like that. After a while, Tut-Tut started to shake. It was cold in the cabin, icy water so close all around, but I knew there was more to Tut-Tut's shaking than the cold.

The roar of the engine changed pitch, rising even higher, and now we started pounding up and down, like we'd hit big waves. Big waves in the canal? I stuck my head out from under the berth and tried to see through the nearest porthole, high above. All I could make out was the driven snow zooming past in streaks of dots and dashes. The bow rose high and came banging down, crashing me into the underside of the berth above. I may even have called out in pain, a call lost in all the roaring and pounding. Tut-Tut was crying silently, his silvery tear tracks the brightest things in the cabin. I mouthed the words "it's all right" to him, but I didn't think he saw. He was back in rough water again, probably his worst nightmare.

On and on we went. I lost track of time but would have guessed that lots had gone by. How far could *Short Sail* go without refueling? The notion that we were headed for Haiti hit me; absolutely crazy, but it made sense in a nasty way. I wondered whether Tut-Tut was thinking the same thing.

All at once the pounding lessened and so did our speed. The hull tilted a bit to the right and *Short Sail* seemed to veer in that direction, making a long curve and then coming to rest—if constant rising and falling, pitching and rolling could be called coming to rest—with the engine idling. Lights shone through the port-holes and then vanished. I heard Borg moving around on deck, and then came voices, not far away.

"Just hold the thing steady," Borg said. The engine shut off, and now I could really hear the storm outside.

Borg grunted once out on the deck, then again, and after that there was just the storm. Even though the en-gine was off, we seemed to be turning, and as we turned, the rising and falling diminished a little, as though we'd found a bit of shelter. Then we just bobbed up and down, almost gently. Music started up, not far away. I could hear the bass—*thump-de-dump-dah, thump-de-dump-dah.*

Things went on like that for some time, and finally I just had to take a peek. I crawled out from under the berth, climbed on top of it, and peered out the porthole. Through the snow, blowing sideways now, I saw noth-ing but the stormy sea, stretching on and on into dark-ness. Way in the distance, the sky was all lit up and pinkish, typical New York nighttime sky.

I turned. Tut-Tut was also kneeling on a berth, but on the opposite side; the port side, actually: nautical lingo was a must on Uncle Joe's boat. The view through Tut-Tut's porthole was very different from mine—no empty ocean, but instead a white wall, rising and rising with no top in sight. A white wall? Someplace way out in the ocean? I didn't understand this at all, but then I noticed a single word written in gold on that white wall: *Boffo*. A memory came: Ashanti and I researching Sheldon Gunn and all the things he owned, including *Boffo,* second-biggest yacht in the world.

Without a word, Tut-Tut and I slipped down and moved silently to the cabin door. We stood and listened, heard no one out there, just the storm and the faint music. My hand, kind of on its own, went to the latch and raised it. I opened the door a few inches. We looked out, saw no one aboard *Short Sail,* snow falling on the deck and on the throttle and all the other instruments on the console.

Tut-Tut and I stepped outside and saw that *Short Sail* was tied to a fold-down platform attached to *Boffo*'s stern. *Boffo* was on the move, but slowly, and towing us behind. Craning my neck to look up, I saw the open ends of three or four decks high above; a rope ladder dangled from the lowest one, reaching all the way down to the platform. There was nobody in sight, and nothing to hear but the storm—quieted down in *Boffo*'s lee—and the music, a little louder now. *Thump-de-dump-dah, thump-de-dump-dah.*

What were the choices? Looking back, I could make out the lit-up nighttime sky of the city but no buildings, not even the tallest towers: we were far from shore.

Could we steal *Short Sail,* somehow ride her all the way back? Yes, I'd been on Uncle Joe's boat—but I'd spent most of my time soaking up rays, not doing any actual driving, didn't even know how to start the engine. We could go back to hiding in the cabin and wait for whatever was going to happen to happen. Or . . .

We stepped over *Short Sail*'s gunwale and onto the platform. I got a grip on the rope ladder, stuck my foot on the first rung, and started up. Ms. Kleinberg had tossed in some rope climbing in one practice, hoping to strengthen our upper bodies. This was like that, only a bit easier because your feet could help out.

I reached the railing of the lowest deck, peered over. The first thing I saw was a gym, a huge one behind glass walls, full of rows and rows of equipment. No one was working out and the only light came from an enormous flat-screen TV on the far wall, showing a sports highlight show. One of those everyday bits of programming: it made me want to be at home, safe in bed.

I looked down the ladder, saw Tut-Tut climbing fast. I stepped over the rail and onto the deck; Tut-Tut vaulted over the railing and landed softly beside me. We started walking forward, the gym on our left. I thought of checking our footprints again, then realized there was no snow on the deck. I bent and touched it, a heated deck, it turned out, that melted the snow away.

We went past the gym, came to an Olympic-size

pool, also glassed-in, surrounded by umbrellas and palm trees; no one swimming or lounging. Tut-Tut and I kept going. The music was louder now, seemed to be floating down from somewhere above. After the swimming pool came a blank wall and then a staircase made of gleaming dark wood. We were standing at its base, unsure about what to do next, when a door opened just a few feet ahead of us and a waiter or steward or whatever you'd call them—he wore black pants and a short white jacket—stepped out with a bottle of champagne in a silver bucket. Had he shot the slightest glance toward the stern, he couldn't have missed us, but instead he turned and walked quickly the other way. Tut-Tut and I went up the stairs.

It turned out to be a graceful curving staircase, with a railing that seemed to be made of crystal. We were almost at the top, meaning the next deck, when the silver heart fluttered for a split second and I heard a voice saying *Hey!* Then came a sound that was kind of like static. It all seemed to be happening in my head and not in the outside world. A moment later the sound went dead.

I turned back to Tut-Tut and whispered, "Did you hear anything?"

"Music," he whispered back.

"Whoa. You're talking?"

His eyes opened wide. "Hey! Th-th-th-th—" He went silent, looked confused. So was I.

We reached the next level, found ourselves in a broad hallway lined with art and flowers. Stormy weather outside, and we were on the cold Atlantic, miles and miles from shore, but it felt like being in some amazing mansion on dry land. We passed what might have been an empty disco, with a stage that was revolving, although no one was on it, and walls that seemed to be made of zebra skins all stitched together. After that we emerged on an open deck with some huge metal sculptures on one side and a row of windows, like portholes but much bigger, on the other. All the portholes were dark except two. I peeked in the first one and saw a cabin, but nothing like the cabin on *Short Sail;* this cabin was huge and luxurious, with antique furniture and a bar that shone with silver and glass. The second lit cabin looked much the same, except for one difference: this one was occupied.

Two men sat across from each other at a delicate-looking little table, gold-trimmed espresso cups between them. The nearest man had a goatee and wore a white robe with one of those Middle Eastern headdresses; the other man was Borg.

Borg said something I couldn't make out: Tut-Tut and I were in the open again, somewhat sheltered from the wind, but it was still blowing hard, driving streamers of snow high over our heads. The Middle Eastern man replied. Borg wrote on a piece of paper, handed it to the Middle Eastern man and left the room by a door on the far side.

The man rose, went to the wall, and took down a picture. There was a safe behind it. He touched a pad with the tip of his finger and the safe swung open. It was a big safe, with three shelves, each one crammed with cash, colorful money on the bottom two shelves and U.S. greenbacks on top. He checked the sheet of paper, then opened a closet beside the safe. Two large suitcases stood inside, fancy French ones—I recognized the logo because Nonna had the same kind. The man pulled the suitcases out of the closet and opened them both. They were each about half full of neatly folded clothes. He took all the clothes from one and transferred them to the other. Then he closed the full suitcase and stuck it back in the closet. After that, he drew the empty suitcase closer to the safe and began filling it with greenbacks, his lips moving like he was keeping silent count. In the end, the suitcase was so jam-packed he had to kneel on it to get it shut. He'd just finished that when a phone rang in the room; I heard it through the glass.

The man rose, crossed the room to a desk, answered the phone. He listened for a moment and hung up. Then he went to the safe, picked up the suitcase and tried to wedge it inside. The safe wasn't big enough. The man carried the suitcase through an archway and into what I could see was a bedroom. He walked out seconds later without the suitcase, closed the safe and left the room.

Footsteps sounded from the direction of the disco. Tut-Tut and I ducked into the sculpture garden or whatever it was and hid behind a steel structure that looked like a flattened-out bear. The waiter, or maybe a different waiter, appeared, bearing an empty silver tray. He walked past the porthole we'd just been looking through and paused before a door. Beside the door was a touchpad, like the one on the safe. The waiter touched it; the door swung in; the waiter entered the room where Borg and the Middle Eastern man had met. The door closed in a slow and automatic way.

Twenty or thirty seconds later, the door opened again and the waiter emerged, now carrying the espresso cups on his silver tray. He headed back toward the disco, the door closing behind him. I didn't think for a moment, just sprinted toward that shrinking space and dove through, Tut-Tut, so skinny, squeezing in behind me. The door closed and made a little click.

It was nice and warm inside. Tut-Tut and I exchanged a glance. "Are you thinking what I'm thinking?" I said.

He nodded, opened the closet, and took out the fancy suitcase, the one filled with clothes. Tut-Tut carried it through the archway and into the bedroom, a very fancy bedroom with a big round bed and mirrored walls. Our images moved back and forth as we searched the room, the movements growing more nervous as time passed. We ended up finding the second suitcase in what should have been the first place we looked, under the bed. Tut-Tut opened it just to be sure. U.S. greenbacks, nothing but hundreds that we could see, a small fortune—or maybe even a big one. We shoved the first suitcase, the one full of clothes, under the bed and took the second one, full of money, back into the main room.

Tut-Tut raised his chin in a now-what look. A good question. The only answer that came to mind—making off, or trying to make off, with *Short Sail*—was one I'd already rejected.

"Um," I said. "Well . . ." And gazed at the suitcase, waiting for an idea. We had all that money, and Silas had the list of all the people who needed it, but how were we—

I felt a tiny pressure in my head, barely there. The silver heart fluttered the tiniest flutter. And then came *Hey!*

I glanced around, my own heart thumping, looking

for the source of that *hey*. It was so clear! But there was only me and Tut-Tut.

"Did you say hey?" I asked him.

"I didn't say anything," Tut-Tut said. "And keep your voice down."

I lowered my voice. "You're talking again," I said, touching his shoulder. "That must mean—"

And then again—*Hey!*—this time followed by another burst of static so loud it hurt my ears, but coming from inside my head, for sure. Then I felt it fully: the power, surging through me. I felt it surging through Tut-Tut, too, could also even see it in a way, just from the expression on his face. I put my glasses away.

Hey! The volume went down on the sound in my head, but the clarity rose, like a radio station tuned in properly. *Hey! Robbie!*

The voice was calling my name?

Do you read me? Come in. Over.

The voice: a dweeby voice, capable of saying dweeby things like *over*.

"Silas," I said. "Yes, I hear you."

Tut-Tut looked at me, amazed and worried, like I was flipping out.

"Don't you hear Silas?" I said.

"No," said Tut-Tut. He glanced around: no Silas in view.

Robbie? Do you read me? If you read me, don't say you read me. Think it! Over.

"Huh?" I said.

Silence.

Huh, I thought.

What do you mean, "huh"? Over.

"What's going on?" Tut-Tut said. "You look funny."

"You don't hear Silas?"

Tut-Tut glanced around. "Silas?"

"He's not here," I said. "But somehow he's—"

What do you mean, "huh"? Over.

Huh means huh. Stop screwing around, Silas—this isn't a good time. What's happening?

Mental telepathy—that's my power! It just came to me. I can communicate by thought and thought alone—who's cooler than me? Oh, yeah—we're on our way. Over.

Who's on their way?

Me and Ashanti. And think "over." You have to think "over" when you get to the end. Like this: over. Over.

I'm not thinking "over." And you don't even know where we are.

How come you're so stubborn? And we don't have to know where you are—we can't go anywhere else.

What do you—

Over. I forgot "over." Over.

For God's sake!

Ow! That hurts my ears. Over.

What do you mean you can't go anywhere else?

There's no steering! Over and out.

Silence.

Silas? Silas?

Nothing.

I turned to Tut-Tut. He was watching me strangely. "They're coming to get us," I said. "Silas and Ashanti."

"Yeah? How?"

"I'm not sure, but Silas can do mental telepathy now."

"And you can do it back to him?" Tut-Tut said.

"I guess so."

"Oh."

Just a little "oh." The idea—a crazy one—came to me that Tut-Tut was jealous. It made no sense, and this was not the time. If they were really coming—but how?— we had to find a safe place to—

The phone rang in the room, same phone that had summoned the Middle Eastern man. It rang six times and then went silent. That expression—danger in the air? I felt the truth of it at that moment.

I picked up the suitcase. Tut-Tut opened the door that led to the deck and the sculpture garden. We stuck our heads out for a quick peek. The coast was clear, maybe the wrong expression, since we were so far from shore. We stepped out, returned to the sculpture garden. Snow fell; wind blew. We sheltered behind the flattened-out bear, sitting together on the suitcase.

"I hope the power stays for a long time," Tut-Tut said.

"Me too."

"Do you think it could stay forever?"

"No."

"Why not?"

Why not? The look in Tut-Tut's eyes made me wish I hadn't said no about the power—especially since I couldn't think of an actual reason. I was fumbling in my mind for some quick fix when I realized we were on the move. Not over the surface of the ocean—that was hard to judge, *Boffo,* so solid and enormous, being more like an island than a ship, plus we had nothing to gauge motion against except snow falling in the night. No, the movement that caught my attention was up. We were rising, no doubt about it, not just Tut-Tut and me, but the whole sculpture garden and the deck beneath it. Up we went, as though on an enormous elevator, slow and silent.

We reached the next deck. Before us stood another glass wall, a glass wall of the smoky kind, that might front a nightclub, for example, not that I'd had any nightclub experience. But what we were gazing into was a nightclub, with little round tables, champagne, cigars, and a jazz combo—piano, bass, guitar, and a beautiful singer in a sparkling gown—on a small stage. She was singing a song I sort of recognized, possibly some old song by Frank Sinatra; my dad was a big fan. Not much of an audience: only two tables were occupied. At one, near the back, sat a few tough-looking guys in black uniforms; some sort of rifle or machine gun—I knew pretty much nothing about guns—hung on its strap from the back of an empty chair. At the other table, front and center, smoking the cigars and drinking the champagne—and not paying any attention to the band, even though they sounded great, the *thump-de-dump-dah, thump-de-dump-dah* of the bass seeming to vibrate through the whole ship—sat two older men in white robes, plus Sheldon Gunn in a black tuxedo. My uncle Joe wears shorts and flip-flops on his boat.

All that, I saw in passing, because we were still going up. The next deck, one from the top, came in view. It was dark, except for one light showing in a long rectangular window. On the other side of the window lay a bowling alley with a single lane. Borg was alone in the bowling alley, sitting at the desk where you keep score. He looked to the side. Someone was coming from that direction: the Middle Eastern man we'd seen in his cabin below.

The Middle Eastern man was carrying the suitcase. He laid it on the scorer's table. Borg made an impatient

278

gesture. The Middle Eastern man started to open the suitcase. From our angle, we couldn't see into it, but had a good view of their faces as they got their first glimpse of the contents.

A good view, but a brief one, on account of how we were still rising. All we caught was initial dawning of their shocked reaction—stunned puzzlement mixed into the Middle Eastern guy's, Borg showing something much uglier—and then they passed from view. The sculpture garden reached the top deck and came to a stop.

Two helicopters sat on the top deck. There were antennas and rotating things, and all sorts of other equipment. Also: no shelter, except a squat steel hutlike structure with tiny windows, through which flowed the only light around. Snow flew sideways; the wind howled; Tut-Tut and I huddled behind the flattened-out bear.

A man emerged from the steel hut wheeling something big on a dolly. Leaning into the wind, he came toward the sculpture garden. He was headed our way! Tut-Tut and I slid around the sculpture, trying to keep it between us and him, but he drew closer and closer. For an instant, he seemed to look right at us. Tut-Tut and I backed quickly out of sight, and kept backing until we were out of the sculpture garden and on the deck. The man stopped by the flattened-out bear and stood the dolly up. Because of the darkness, or all the snow, he hadn't seen us. We ducked behind the steel hut.

And then the sculpture garden was on the move again, going down. At the same time, the lights in the hut went out, and the darkness deepened. Tut-Tut was shivering inside his hoodie, snow all down his neck. I was cold, too, that strange warm period long past.

"Tut-Tut?"

"Y-y-y-yeah?"

My heart went *bang-bang* in my chest. "Are you all right?"

"Could be warmer," he said.

Whew. That last little stutter was just from the cold: for a moment I'd thought we were losing the power.

"How about we go inside?" he said.

With a grunt, he opened the thick steel door of the hut. We went inside. The only light came from an in-strument panel. I saw another dolly, some boxes, and a steep metal staircase descending into darkness. What choice did we have? I got a good grip on the suitcase, put my foot on the first step; and as I did a horrible *bwa-da bwa-da* alarm went off, very loud, like in a prison movie when they find out that what's sleeping on the inmate's bunk is a bundle of clothes.

I froze. *BWA-DA! BWA-DA!* Then a radio crackled over by the instrument panel. "All hands! All hands! Suspected intruders on board! All hands!"

"Hurry!" I said. We had to get down the ladder, find some hideout deep inside the ship. I felt with my foot for the next step. A light went on down below, followed by the sound of running footsteps.

I jumped back up to floor level.

A man's voice rose up the staircase. "Whoever it is, we want them alive."

BWA-DA! BWA-DA!

I threw open the door of the steel hut. We raced outside. The wind was shrieking. The snow blinded me now; I could barely see the dim shape of the nearest helicopter. We ran to it, hoping for a hiding place. Lights flashed back on in the hut and then men came pouring onto the deck.

Hey! You guys around? Over.

Silas? *Silas! Silas!*

A searchlight went on, the beam sweeping toward us. Tut-Tut and I were holding hands; I wasn't sure when that had started. In my other hand, I still gripped the suitcase. We scrambled away from the searchlight beam, which almost reached us as it swept by. The men were coming, big dark shapes behind the screen of flying whiteness. Tut-Tut and I backed away and backed away until we had nowhere to go.

We stood on the edge of *Boffo*'s top deck—a top deck that had no rail—high above an ice-cold ocean we couldn't even see. I peered into the storm.

Silas! Silas!
No response.
Silas! Silas! Over!
But nothing.
On deck, a man shouted. "Do you see something?"
And another shouted, "Where?"
"There!"
A machine gun fired. *Ack-ack-ack. Ack-ack-ack.* And a stream of hot light shot through the night, but nowhere near us. Then another gun joined in, much closer, firing on and on, shooting another stream of bullets aimed in an arc just like the searchlight, coming closer and closer. We darted sideways, or tried to, but we lost our footing on the slippery deck, losing it at the same instant that the wind rose up to a whole new level. With one enormous gust, it blew us right off the deck and into the night.

For a long moment, we seemed to hang there, hovering in the air, actually above deck level. Through the scrim of snow, I could even make out Borg and Sheldon Gunn yelling at each other by the hut. No one on deck was looking up.

I still had the suitcase. The thought of taking all that money to the bottom was kind of comforting. We started our plunge.

26

Tut-Tut and I held hands tight. I was aware of that, and of the fact that his eyes were closed and his face seemed calm, and that his dreads were pointing straight up, but I knew nothing else, except that I had a monstrous terror inside, ready to swell up into something way bigger than me. It made me want to scream and scream; I tried my hardest not to. Then, through a little break in the snow, I glimpsed the ocean, with its towering white-capped waves, coming up so fast, and the terror monster hit the screaming button. Before I could actually let out that first scream, I heard Silas, not a thought message, but his actual voice, high and squeaky and barely audible through the storm and the roar of the sea.

"Hang on!"

We plunged. Two enormous waves crashed together, sending a jet of spray high enough to hit my face. And just as it did, a hand reached out of all the blowing snow and grabbed onto Tut-Tut's shoulder. Then came a sudden lurch and we leveled out, skimming over the ragged wave tops so low that I got soaked from my hand—the one holding on to Tut-Tut—all the way to my shoulder. We rose slightly and I saw Silas, very strange-looking in a one-piece ski suit and a tasseled ski hat, now grasping Tut-Tut's free hand. With his other hand, he held on to Ashanti. She flashed me a big grin.

"Don't blame me," she said. "I was out hours ago, but Silas got lost in the basement of his own building."

"Not lost," Silas said. "More disoriented."

We soared, the four of us stretched out in a line and holding hands—me, Tut-Tut, Silas, Ashanti—ten or fifteen feet above the sea; a sea that sounded angry to me, like it had been cheated.

"Can we take this a little higher?" Silas said.

"It does what it does," Ashanti said.

"Good enough for me," Tut-Tut said.

"Hey," said Ashanti. "Will you listen to him."

Tut-Tut smiled.

And then we did rise a bit, maybe another twenty feet. Up ahead loomed *Boffo*'s huge form. Lights were going on all over the ship. A voice from up high called out, "What's that? A paraglider?"

A searchlight flashed on and the beam came probing

toward us, sweeping by just over our heads. We swerved around *Boffo,* but way too slowly and way too close; I saw a man running across one of the lower decks with a rifle in each hand, and then the beam arced by again, missing by only a few feet.

Meanwhile the four of us—Ashanti slightly out front and doing the towing—moved in a gentle curve around the boat, rising gradually, and then straightened out, the city glowing in the distance. I glanced back at *Boffo:* up on the top deck, figures swarmed around one of the helicopters.

We soared toward land, the wind at our backs, or actually at the soles of our feet, since we were horizontal, our bodies parallel to the sea below.

"What's in the suitcase?" Ashanti said.

"Casheroo," I said. "Have you got your list, Silas?"

"Does the bear poop in the woods?"

"Just a simple yes or no."

"Yes."

"Good," I said. "That means we can—"

A helicopter roared up into the sky off *Boffo's* top deck. At first it took off in the wrong direction, out to sea. Then it veered left and came circling back.

"Can't we go faster?" Silas said.

"You know the answer to that," Ashanti said.

The helicopter tilted hard, the blades going *thwap-*

thwap-thwap, and shot right over us, but high above, a light on the front casting a long narrow beam. *Just keep going.* But the helicopter did not keep going; instead it veered left again and started another circle, swooping lower this time. I saw what was happening.

Power, make us invisible.

We remained visible. The helicopter swung in a wide turn, farther out to sea, then returned, flying lower now, almost down to our level.

Power, make us invisible. Over.

We remained visible. I looked back. The bright narrow light zoomed toward us, closer and closer. *Thwap-thwap-thwap* filled the night, even drowning out the storm.

"Silas! Use your telepathy!"

"To do what?"

"Something, for God's sake!" I glanced at the silver heart on my—but no: the silver heart—the whole bracelet, was gone. The sea had torn it away. My heart pounded. I came close to crying out in despair. Then I realized we hadn't crashed. Why not? If we'd lost the power, why were we still soaring? Why was my vision still perfect without my glasses?

THWAP-THWAP-THWAP. The helicopter's beam homed in, closer and closer, and now its fuzzy outer edge reached us and—

And then a huge bird—an owl, snowy white, but could owls really be so big?—emerged from all that snow, kind of like a bird version of the storm itself, and flew right by us. Did owls come out to sea? This one did. It seemed to watch me for a second or two, and I thought I knew this owl: the one with the strange washed-out blue eyes. It glided between us and the helicopter, appearing in silhouette not unlike a paraglider. The light beam passed over the owl's wings, just for a split second, but someone in the helicopter must have caught a quick glimpse of something, because it veered sharply away from us and took off after the owl.

Some kind of gun started firing from the helicopter, the orange tracks of the bullets cutting through the blowing snow. The owl soared higher, out of range of the helicopter's searchlight. The helicopter rose, too, the searchlight probing higher and higher, but it shone only on blowing snow and dark night. The shooting went on and on—*ACK-ACK, ACK-ACK.* The helicopter made a circle, moving out to sea, and then another, each circle farther away and less certain, and either the shooting had stopped or it was too distant to hear. I thought I heard a far-off *hoot-hoot,* but it might have been the storm.

We soared on, the wind starting to lose some of its force at last, the snow falling not quite so hard. The towers of Manhattan appeared, and then the bridges, all lit up, and the harbor. The Statue of Liberty, too, was lit, the torch shining bright. We glided right by her face, so strong and beautiful.

Snow lay thick all over the city. The streets were buried, the rooftops white—no traffic, no people. Silas took out his list. We crossed the river, soared through the streets of Brooklyn, hovering by every doorway on the list long enough for Tut-Tut and me to open the suitcase, count out a bundle of money, and make a deposit.

The night slipped by, snow falling lightly, the wind just the odd gust, and the city quiet. The sky was beginning to lighten in the east when we came to Your Thai, last in the mind of the power, if the power had a mind. Mr. Nok was clearing snow from the stairwell. He opened up and went inside.

We hovered by the door. I opened the suitcase. Tut-Tut scooped out the last of the money and shoved it through the letter slot. Mr. Nok must have heard the sound. He turned and moved toward the money, his eyes opening wide. Mr. Nok looked out, but not up, so he missed us, on the rise.

"Where are we going?" Silas said. "I'm sleepy."

No one answered. No one knew. We glided over the snowy streets at first-floor level. The canal came in sight. As we passed over it, only a foot or two above the surface, turning sickly green as the light grew stronger, I let go of the empty suitcase. It landed without a splash and disappeared.

"Th-th-th-th-," said Tut-Tut.

I glanced his way in alarm. At the same time, my vision started to blur.

"Uh-oh," said Ashanti.

We thumped down heavily in the snow on the far side of the canal, just yards from the Red Goat. Or at least I thought it was the Red Goat, with my vision all screwy. I rose, dusted off the snow, put on my glasses. Yes, the Red Goat.

"N-n-n-n-," Tut-Tut said.

"No power," said Silas.

"It lasted just long enough," said Ashanti.

Maybe, I thought, but not for Tut-Tut. He saw me looking at him, shrugged his shoulders, smiled a little smile.

"We should all give that silver heart a kiss," Ashanti said.

"This thing is . . ." I said, and held up my bare wrist.

"Oh, my God! When did that happen?"

I told them.

"So what does this mean?" Ashanti said. "The power's in you now?"

"I don't know," I said.

"We could run some tests," Silas said.

"Some other time," I told him. "Let's go home."

We started walking through the snow. Soon a plow came along and we followed it, but other than that one plow, we had the streets of Brooklyn to ourselves. No one spoke: we were all way too tired. First Silas peeled off, then—near HQ, not his apartment—Tut-Tut, and finally Ashanti. She took out her key. "My dad's out of town, and my mom never gets up before eleven." Ashanti gave me a look. "You did good."

"Thatcha," I said.

"Comin' atcha," said Ashanti. She went inside.

I came to the alley, followed it toward the opening that led to our back yard. The ladder was still down, exactly as I'd left it. I climbed up to the platform outside our downstairs bathroom window—dragging my feet, now so heavy—pulled the ladder after me, laid it down in its place. Looking back, I noticed the clear track of my footprints in the yard. Nothing I could do about it but hope that the snow, still drifting down, would fall a little longer.

I climbed to the next level, reached my bedroom window, open a crack the way I'd left it. I got my hands under the frame and pushed up. Nothing happened. I bent my legs, put my whole body into it. No use. I was too tired, or maybe not strong enough to begin with. The window was frozen stuck. All of a sudden, I felt close to tears. I'd come so close!

I was considering smashing the glass and inventing

some stupid story, when, with a wag-wag of his tail, Pendleton appeared on the other side of the glass. My heart lifted, just from the sight of him. No way that Pendleton could actually do anything to—

Then, without a word or gesture on my part, Pendleton stuck his muzzle in the crack and raised his head in a single strong motion. The window slid up. I climbed inside and closed it. The house was silent.

"Pendleton," I said in a low voice. "Is the power in you?"

How was that possible?

I gave him a big hug. He licked my face.

A minute or two later, I was under the covers, Pendleton beside me, hogging most of the bed.

When I woke up, Pendleton was gone. I put on my glasses, hurried to the window, and looked out. It was still snowing—very lightly, just the occasional flake, but: no tracks.

I went downstairs, found Mom and Dad relaxing in front of the TV, shoulders touching, both of them in jeans and sweatshirts. This did not look normal.

"Good morning, sleepyhead," said Mom.

"Make that afternoon," Dad said. "But there's no school tomorrow, in case you're worried about getting your homework done."

"Why not?"

"The mayor declared a snow day," Mom said.

My dad gave me funny glance. "You haven't looked outside, Robbie? The whole city's shut down."

I peered through the window, pretended to be stunned.

"Nice to see you wearing your glasses," Mom said. "They're really very stylish."

"And even if they aren't," said Dad, "you'll be eligible for contacts in—"

Mom held up her hand. "Here he is now," she said.

"Who?" I asked.

"Your buddy."

Uh-oh. "Who's my buddy?"

"Sheldon Gunn," said Mom. "Just being facetious."

Didn't know that word. Had Mom figured something out? I gave her a quick glance, detected no hidden meaning. I moved closer to the TV, took a look at Sheldon Gunn.

". . . and so," he was saying, "in light of current market conditions, we have taken the prudent decision to postpone the enactment of the New Brooklyn Redevelopment Project at this time." He stepped away from the mic.

The reporter—Dina DiNunzio, I remembered her hard face and fluffy hair—shoved the mic back in his face and said, "Is it true, Mr. Gunn, that you've had a major falling out with your Saudi financiers?"

"Absolutely not. Prince Abdul and I remain the clos-est of friends."

"What about these reports that you raised the rents on hundreds of Brooklyn tenants to drive them out and clear the way for the project, but that some business ri-vals managed to get those rents paid in the hope of later taking over the redevelopment of Brooklyn themselves?"

Sheldon Gunn paused. His eyes appeared to hood over. "You seem to know more than I do, Dina. Have these so-called business rivals got a name?"

"I'm asking you, sir."

"I have no reason to believe there's the slightest truth in your hypothesis," Gunn said.

"There are also rumors that some sort of anonymous Robin Hood type is the source of all this rent money."

"Complete fiction," said Gunn. "And let me add that my organization has the highest possible reputation when it comes to landlord-tenant relations. We've won the Mayor's Cup ten years in a row."

"But—"

Gunn moved away.

Mom's phone rang. She answered, listened, said, "Really?" And then. "Oh." She hung up and rose. "Have to go into work," she said.

"Now?" said Dad.

"Emergency department meeting," Mom said. "Gunn fired us, as of today. He wants his fees back, going all the way to last May. And Egil Borg got the ax. It sounds like chaos."

Mom went to work. Later on TV came a brief report about a convicted arsonist named Harry Henkel who was under arrest but refusing to talk. Not long after that, Dad sent me to Your Thai to pick up some dinner. Mr. Nok looked very happy. He was running a special on just about everything.

Mr. Nok's special was still happening on Saturday. I picked up four cartons of *kaeng phet ped yang* and some sodas and we met at HQ. Kind of cold inside—there was still plenty of snow on the ground. Silas reported that Heinz Mott had surfaced with a new blog called How Now Sheldon Gunn dot-com. We proposed some toasts—like "Here's to *Boffo*"—and gobbled up every scrap from the cartons.

"Do you think the power will ever come back?" Silas said.

"First there has to be injustice," I said.

"Plenty of that around," said Ashanti.

"Y-y-y-y-ye-ye-ye-," said Tut-Tut, and kept trying and trying until he finally got to "Yes!"

"Here's to justice," I said.

We clinked soda cans.